THE RADCLIFFE LEGACY

AND

OTHER OXFORD STORIES

OxPens

www.oxpens.co.uk

This, the fifth volume of short stories from Oxpens local authors visits Oxford in four different centuries, from the 18th to the present day. History interweaves with story-telling, fantasy with reality and some tales are decidedly ghostly, whether rooted in the Ashmolean Museum or the Rollright Stones near Chipping Norton. Where was the infamous Cutteslowe Wall? What don't the estate agents tell you about moving into North Oxford? Read on ...

Dedicated to the memory of
Ray Peirson

15.12.1947 to 19.11.2015

A valued previous contributor
and dear friend.

Copyright © Contributors 2017

This book is sold subject to the condition that it shall not, by way of trade or otherwise, be lent, resold, hired out, converted to another format or otherwise circulated without the publishers' prior conjunction in any other format other than that in which it is published.

The moral rights of the contributors are asserted as the writers.

ISBN 978-1-910779-37-8

The cover image is by Valerie Petts and is reproduced by kind permission of the artist.

These stories are works of fiction and the characters and events in them exist only in these pages and in the authors' imagination

Print edition and eBook
typeset and published by
Oxford eBooks Ltd.
www.oxford-ebooks.com

Oxford eBooks

COLIN DEXTER

29.9.1930 to 21.3.2017

As this volume was in preparation, we were greatly saddened to hear of the death of friend and unofficial patron of OxPens Publishing, Colin Dexter. Famous for his 'Morse' books, his status as one of our best known writers didn't prevent him from being tremendously kind to new authors. He admitted to being pleasantly surprised at the high quality of the work produced by the Oxford Writers' Group, and supported our OxPens anthologies from the beginning, as well as many of us individually, speaking at our launches and providing thoughtful quotes for our books. Even in declining health, he made a point of attending our parties, never failing to entertain the company with his fund of amusing stories. He was a kind friend who was always generous with his time. He will be much missed.

Contents

Foreword	Ann Granger	1
The Danger of Wishes	Angela Reid	3
Through the Cutteslowe Wall	Heather Rosser	15
Malachi Stilt-Jack	John Kitchen	25
The Radcliffe Legacy	Linora Lawrence	35
The Day the Snow Fell	Ben McSeoin	47
Along for the Ride	Margaret Pelling	57
Home for Christmas	Jane Stemp	69
A Cup of Coffee	Gina Claye	73
The Witching Stones	Liz Harris	83
Seventh Heaven	Rosie Orr	93
The Vegetarian Dog	Andrew Puckett	101
To Hades Via Carfax	Radmilla May	107
The Woodcut	Paul W. Nash	119
The Blenheim Deception or What you Will	Sylvia Vetta	131
Cat Amongst the Pigeons	Mark Davies	141
Flying with the Angels	Jane Gordon-Cumming	151
Welcome to North Oxford	Alison Honey	157
About the Authors		165

Ann Granger is the acclaimed crime writer of no less than 4 separate series of crime fiction: *Mitchell & Markby, Fran Varady, Campbell and Carter* and her current series, the *Lizzie Martin Mysteries* which are set in Victorian London. Her most recent publication is *The Dead Woman of Deptford* and coming later in 2017 will be *Rooted in Evil*.

Foreword

Think of Oxford. Now try to imagine how many stories are secreted within its mediaeval nooks and crannies; the world-within-worlds of its famous colleges; and in its more modern institutions. Here is a fine collection of new tales, all with an Oxford or Oxfordshire setting, and all from writers with strong connections to the city.

Did you have a kaleidoscope when you were a child? I did and would peer into its glittering depths spellbound. Each time I picked it up, it rewarded me with a new and dazzling array of colour and interconnected shapes. Then, at a tap of a finger, the pieces reformed to create a different but no less fascinating pattern. So each author of a story in this book has taken the handful of pieces and cast them into a different mould. Each one is different, a surprise, and each will take you on a delightful journey.

Let no one doubt the skill required to master the art of the short story. It calls on all the basic needs of a full-length novel. There must be a 'proper' plot. The characters must be believable (no matter how fantastic). The reader should long to know what is going to happen to them. The setting must be realistic. Above all, it should inspire that momentary suspension of disbelief that transports the reader into a fictional world without a stumble along the way. And all this in a couple of thousand words!

I have written some forty or so full length novels but I have approached the writing of none of them with the trepidation that composing a short story would inspire in me! So I salute all contributors to this volume and invite the readers to enter its multi-faceted and absorbing world.

Ann Granger

The Radcliffe Legacy & Other Oxford Stories

THE DANGER OF WISHES

ANGELA REID

It is already almost dark as Isabel runs up the steps and through the revolving glass door into the Ashmolean Museum. Behind her the rain splatters onto the pavement and the reflected light from the nearby street lamps fractures and shivers under the onslaught. Isabel pauses for a moment allowing time for her eyes to adjust to the bright whiteness inside, and for her heart to steady. Shaking the water from the folds of her umbrella she tucks it into the nearby stand.

'We'll be closing in an hour,' says a male voice from behind her.

Isabel spins round to find herself confronted by a slightly built young man, a museum security pass hangs from his neck. She forces a reassuring smile to her lips.

'Oh, I will be long gone by then. I am meeting my husband.' Her voice breaks as she adds, 'He should be here… very soon.'

The young man looks at her sympathetically. 'You look done in, madame. Why don't you check out the Egyptian galleries while you're waiting? They're awesome. Do you know those Egyptians believed every word they wrote, or spoke, had some sort of magical power?'

Isabel shakes her head.

'So,' the young man continues, 'if you want your husband to get here soon, say so, mean it, and he'll be here before you know it.'

Isabel smiles and says obediently, and firmly, 'My husband will be here soon.'

The young man gives her an approving nod and heads towards the escalator.

But will Robert be here soon? Once a rugged bear of a

man, recently he has shrunk into himself, his shoulders forming a hesitant stoop, his confident smile just a shadowed memory. Sometimes she wonders if he really still is the man she married fifteen years ago.

Isabel makes her way towards a sign directing her to 'Egypt at its Origins'. She has never been to Egypt. Robert spent several months travelling up the Nile with his first girlfriend, an Egyptology student, but he has never wanted to return.

The recently refurbished museum is all steel and glass and light. As she drifts through the Egyptian gallery, Isabel's attention is caught by a framed papyrus propped up in a display case. The scene glows gold and amber. She tries to make sense of it. The drawing is skilled and intricate. Figures fill a large hall; some are human, others are part animal. One particularly strange crouching creature catches her attention. At first glance it looks rather like a peculiar breed of dog, but on closer inspection she sees it has the head of a crocodile and a body that seems to be half hippopotamus and half big cat. She is fascinated.

She rests her fingers lightly on the glass. If only Robert would change his mind about returning to Egypt. The thought of Robert makes her stomach twist. She checks her watch. It is nearly half past four. How long does it take to sign your life away? No time at all. Isabel pulls out her mobile. No texts. No missed calls.

A light touch on her shoulder makes her spin round. Robert is behind her.

'Goodness, you startled me. I was just wishing you were here, and here you are.'

Robert's mouth twists into a bitter smile. 'Be careful what you wish for. I wished David would come back and make his peace with Mother and look what happened.'

'The law of unintended consequences,' agrees Isabel trying to read Robert's expression. He looks tired, beaten.

But she has to ask.

'So what did the solicitor say?'

Robert sighs. 'It's no go, I'm afraid.'

'So we lose the house.' It is a statement, not a question. Yet Greenacres is far more than a house, it is Robert's childhood home. Isabel has grown to love every brick of the old farmhouse. It perches half hidden by the beech woods, right on the edge of the Chiltern escarpment. From the window seat in the sitting room, on a clear day, she can see right across the Thames plain to the distant blue of the Cotswold hills.

'I can't bear it, Robert. I know you love it even more than I do. How can we live somewhere else?'

Robert takes Isabel's hand. 'I am so glad Mother asked us to move in with her all those years ago.'

Isabel rests her head on Robert's shoulder. 'Me too. I loved your mother, even though looking after her hasn't always been easy. But how we hated that cramped flat in the Cowley Road.'

'Instead the boys have spent their childhood in a beautiful, old house with plenty of space, a garden to play football in, and woods for exploring.' Robert gazes into the distance as he speaks. 'Nothing can take those memories away.'

Suddenly Isabel realises he doesn't just look tired, he looks old. She stares at the ceiling, fighting the tears pricking her eyes. Seeing Robert like that is the worst thing of all. She feels a deep fury begin to build inside her. It's all David's fault. How dare he walk into their lives, and without a qualm, change everything?

She had never met David. For longer than she had known Robert, David had been in Australia. He went there as soon as he finished school, apparently working on some sheep station in the middle of nowhere. Travel had never appealed to Robert. How could two brothers be so different? The only contact from David had been the annual Christmas card addressed to his mother, which she dropped unopened into the recycling bin.

It had been a glorious golden day in autumn, when Isabel decided the time had come to start pruning back the roses. She was in the front garden, with Musket, her mother-in-law's black and white springer spaniel, as a battered and rusting Volkswagen Golf clattered into the driveway. As soon as the driver climbed out of the car, Isabel had known that he must be David. He was almost identical to Robert, only a few inches taller and a few inches slimmer. His jacket was threadbare and patched at the elbows, his shirt collar was fraying and his shoes had obviously been mended more than once.

He was not alone. An elf-like child with chestnut curls and eyes like dark woodland pools, climbed out of the back seat, carrying a small posy of wild flowers.

'You must be Robert's wife,' David held out his hand. His grip was firm. 'I'm David.'

A man who likes his own way, thought Isabel. 'Your mother will be thrilled to see you,' she said, more in hope than belief. 'She's in her bedroom. Robert's with her.'

Indeed, neither Maria or Robert seemed particularly thrilled to see David.

Maria fixed her eldest son with an icy stare. 'So you have deigned to visit me at last.'

'Oh Mother,' he said kneeling by her bedside and kissing her hand in what Isabel thought was an overly theatrical way. 'It's wonderful to see you. Please forgive me for not coming sooner. Tickets home are so expensive.'

Maria snatched her hand away. 'That's as may be. Who is this child?'

David gave her a sharp look as he pulled the girl forward. 'This is Camille, of course. My daughter.' He looked around the room. 'I don't see any of the photos I sent you with my

Christmas cards.'

Maria glared at her son. 'It wasn't cards I wanted from you.'

Before David could reply, Camille fixed her dark eyes on her grandmother, saying gravely. 'I have always wanted to meet you, and now I have. I am so happy.' Then laying the posy carefully on the bed, she flung her arms around Maria's neck.

Maria looked startled but not entirely displeased. She removed the arms surprisingly gently whilst saying brusquely, 'Aah, yes, quite. It is good to meet you too, Camille.'

Isabel could see a softness behind Maria's eyes that she had never seen before.

'So how old are you?' Maria asked.

'I'm nearly eight,' replied Camille, her eyes fixed on her grandmother.

'And where's your mother?' Maria asked briskly.

'In heaven. That's what Daddy says.'

Isabel felt the shock in the room at the child's words. She glanced at David.

His face was hard. 'Nicole died last year. A car accident. I did tell you in the last Christmas card.'

Maria ignored him, her eyes remaining on her granddaughter. 'I'm sorry about your mother.' There was an awkward pause before she asked, 'So where do you live?'

'Forever away,' replied Camille, her eyes wide and sad.

David's eyes rested on his daughter and his face relaxed. 'Camille's right. Home is forever away from everywhere. It's outside Two Rivers, Western Australia. But the simple life suits us just fine.' He switched his gaze to Robert. 'We will be flying back at the end of next month. I still hate the thought of cold British winters.'

Isabel could almost smell the relief that flooded the room. The alien presence was just here for a visit. Nothing had changed.

'You will stay here tonight,' commanded Maria, her eyes on Camille.

So David and Camille stayed, but not just for the night. Over the following weeks David was outside mowing the lawn and weeding the flower beds, or he was inside reading to Maria from *War and Peace*, her favourite novel, while Camille played endlessly with Musket in the garden. The spaniel would chase her, she would chase him, and they would end up in a laughing, barking heap on the grass.

'I love all animals,' she would say wrapping her arms tightly round his neck, 'but I love Musket best in the whole wide world.'

Thus Isabel, while the boys were at school, could rediscover the long forgotten freedom of meeting up with friends for lunch, and going on shopping expeditions. She began to warm to David.

Robert was more suspicious. He remembered how his brother used to think only of himself. Surely there was an ulterior motive for this charm offensive. One day he cornered David and demanded the truth. Why was he really here? Was it about their mother's will?

'We are happy in Australia as we are,' insisted David, 'I just wanted to say goodbye to Mother and for Camille to meet her. I know how much you and Isabel have done for our mother, and you deserve everything you will get.'

Gradually the frost between the brothers began to thaw, but it was Camille who turned spring into summer enchanting them all with her wide-eyed gaze and her gentle ways.

When eventually David and Camille left for several weeks of exploring Britain before they flew home, the house felt uncomfortably empty. It was on the following Thursday that Maria suffered a fatal heart attack. David and Camille returned to Greenacres the next day. Isabel watched in disbelief as this time David drove up the long, leafy drive in a gleaming silver BMW Hatchback, wearing a suit that was undoubtedly Savile Row. She was about to say something, when John Peabody, the family solicitor arrived.

She and Robert then listened incredulously as he explained that Maria had left everything to be split equally between her sons.

'Everything?' Robert demanded, 'including this house?' His mouth was tight with shock mixed with fury. He turned on his brother. 'Did you know about this?'

David smiled a wide, white smile. 'Yes, dearest brother, I did.'

'You lied to Robert,' snapped Isabel feeling like she wanted to throw up. 'You told him you didn't want a share of her estate, that he deserved all he'd get.'

'Well,' smirked David, 'he does deserve what he'll get, that's half of everything.'

Robert was studying his immaculately dressed brother. 'But it wasn't about the money, was it? You were always jealous of me.'

David glared at him. 'Mother's little darling,' he sneered, 'You're right, it wasn't the money.'

'I was going to say that the change in the will meant neither you nor I would live here because neither of us has the money to buy the other out.' Robert shook his head. 'But I'm guessing that's not true?'

David smiled an even wider, whiter, smile. 'I just wanted to even things up a little.' He fixed Robert with a look laden with years of brotherly envy. 'Remember it was my home too.'

'But you live a simple life in the outback,' Isabel was still trying to make sense of his words, his smart suit and his even smarter car.

David shrugged. 'It's true, we do live simply in the outback, but I own five thousand square miles of it.'

Robert was grim-faced. 'You set out to deceive us. You turned up looking like a tramp, and told us you could hardly afford the airfare. All so you could wheedle your way into our mother's will.'

David shrugged. 'Just because I arrived in an old suit and an even older car, you all assumed I was poor. And I never said I couldn't afford the airfares, I just stated they were expensive. Travelling First Class always is.'

A door slams somewhere deep in the Ashmolean bringing Isabel back to the present. She cannot believe that there is really no hope at all. 'Aren't there any grounds for saying she was of unsound mind?'

Robert gives a sharp, bitter laugh. 'Come on, Mother was as sharp as a knife, right to the end.'

'But she was taken in by him.'

'Weren't we all! And he did nothing illegal. I did check with the solicitor about that.' Robert closes his eyes and his mouth twists as if he is in physical pain. 'I should have seen his game. I should have sent him packing that first day.'

Isabel squeezes his hand. 'So you signed.'

Robert sighs. 'At least if David and Camille have Greenacres, it stays in the family.'

Anger at how they had been deceived, bubbles and boils inside her. It is a strange and uncomfortable feeling. There is a long silence. The gallery is silent too. Most people have already headed for the exit. The museum must be closing shortly.

Slowly she becomes aware that Robert is staring intently at the display cabinet in front of them.

'That papyrus shows the Weighing of the Heart ceremony,' he adds bitterly, 'I guess David's heart would weigh pretty heavily.'

Isabel is prepared to be distracted. It will give her a chance to regain control of her feelings. 'What do you mean?'

Robert hesitates as if searching the furthest corners of his memory. 'When an ancient Egyptian died, their body was mummified so that they could inhabit it again in the afterlife. I think organs like the lungs and the brain were removed, but the heart was important to their journey into the afterlife. It was left in the body so it could be weighed in the Hall of Judgement. If during their lifetime they had been good their heart would be light, but if they had been bad, then their heart would be heavy.'

Isabel studies the scene for a moment. 'The weight of evil,' she murmurs, then adds, 'I can see a heart on one side of the scales, but why's there a feather on the other?'

'That's the feather of Ma'at,' explains Robert, 'she's the goddess of truth and justice. If the heart weighs more than the feather, then the person can't pass into the afterlife.' He points at the strange creature crouching by the scales. 'Instead, the monstrous Ammut devours the evil heart, and the person is consigned to eternal darkness.'

Isabel stares at the heart on the scale. Robert's right. David's heart would certainly be heavier than the feather. Hate seeps like ice water through Isabel's body. If only he were dead…

As the thought fills her mind the papyrus seems suddenly clearer, as if she is seeing it properly for the first time. The colours are more vivid, and somewhere, far away, there's the sound of chanting. The figures appear to tremble with life, the smell of burning oil and ancient dust fills the air. As a camera focuses in on a close up, Isabel's gaze is drawn to the heart lying on the scales. No longer black and desiccated, it pulsates blood red, and glistens in the light of flaming torches.

As Isabel watches, the scales move, and the heart plunges earthwards, while the white feather of Ma'at spins into the air. A jackal-headed figure raises his arm and Ammut opens his great crocodile mouth. Isabel has a glimpse of rows of deadly pointed teeth before Ammut leaps towards the waiting heart, which vanishes down the creature's throat.

'Isabel, come on, stop day dreaming. It's time to go.'

Robert's voice brings Isabel back to reality. She shivers suddenly as she remembers the security guard's words about the ancient Egyptians' belief in the power of words and thoughts. As she and Robert make their way out of the Ashmolean into the wet, winter's evening, and head towards St Giles and their car, she tells herself firmly that it is all nonsense.

It is May. The air in University Parks is heavy with the sweet smell of freshly mown grass. Isabel sits on a bench beside the River Cherwell, enjoying the sunshine and watching a group of students trying to control their punts, an activity involving much laughing and splashing. Musket is lying in a patch of sunlight at her feet, chasing rabbits in his sleep. She can hardly believe it is six months since they had left Greenacres. Living in Oxford has taken some getting used to, but she is enjoying the freedom she now has. Gone are the endless hours of school runs, now the boys walk to school. Gone are the hours of gardening, instead a morning a week keeps their tiny garden immaculate. Now she meets friends for coffee or lunch at will, and particularly enjoys regular visits to Oxford's theatres and museums, all within walking distance of the Victorian gem that is their new home.

Occasionally she has thought about that strange moment in the Ashmolean in the dark days of last winter. For weeks afterwards she had wondered apprehensively if she would hear that David had died suddenly, and now experiences a wave of guilt ridden amazement that she had ever felt that much hate for anyone.

She closes her eyes and leans back enjoying the sun on her face. David and Camille are probably already installed at Greenacres for the summer, and Isabel realises she no longer minds. She is more content than she has been for years.

The peace is shattered by the furious vibrating of the

mobile in her jacket pocket. She doesn't recognise the number.

'Is that you, Isabel?' demands the voice. 'It's Grahame Chandler here, from the Lodge below Greenacres. I apologise for phoning you out of the blue like this, but I had to warn you.'

Isabel feels her stomach churn. 'Warn me about what?'

She remembers Grahame all too well. He is one of those people who knows the answers to everything.

'Something terrible has happened.'

Isabel's mouth is dry, the palms of her hands are sweating. 'To David?'

'How did you know?'

'Just a guess. Tell me.'

'He was hit by the lorry. He didn't have a chance. The police are on their way, and the ambulance, but I know he's dead.'

Isabel clutches the phone to her ear. Her thoughts swirl. It's just a terrible coincidence. It must be. 'I don't understand,' she manages, 'what lorry?'

Grahame continues as if she hasn't spoken. 'I was in my garden. I heard the child running and calling out.'

Dread clutches at Isabel's lungs. She can't breathe. 'A child running? You mean Camille's involved?'

'I'm sorry.' Grahame's voice is little more than a whisper.

'You said she was calling out?'

'For Musket. She was trying to get him to come back.'

She glances down at the spaniel sleeping at her feet. 'But Musket is here with me, in Oxford.'

There is a longer pause. 'I'm so sorry.'

'Stop saying you're sorry. Tell me what's happened.' Isabel forces the words through frozen lips. Her body is shaking uncontrollably.

'David must have been chasing after her. To stop her before she reached the road, I guess. I reached the gate just in time to see the lorry hit them both. They didn't stand a chance. I couldn't stop it happening, I couldn't...'

Isabel feels ice where her heart should be. It must just be a terrible coincidence. Anything else was impossible. She had never wished Camille any harm. Never.

There is a long silence. For a moment Isabel thinks Grahame has disconnected, then he speaks. His voice is tentative, as if the words are being forced from him, 'There is one odd thing though. The lorry driver is going on and on about some weird dog-like creature crossing the road. He keeps saying if he hadn't been watching that, he would have seen the child and David. He would have braked in time.'

THROUGH THE CUTTESLOWE WALL

HEATHER ROSSER

There was a shuffling of feet as the bell announced the end of the day at Cutteslowe School.

'Put your books in your desk, pick up your gas masks from under your chairs and stand up straight.'

Miss Armstrong surveyed the pinched faces of the girls and boys in front of her. It was coming up to their second Christmas of the war and the privations were beginning to take their toll.

As was the custom at the end of the school day she said a brief prayer for their safety that night and for the troops fighting for freedom in far-flung places.

'You may go now,' she said and watched with satisfaction as the pupils filed out of the classroom in an orderly fashion. She knew she was fortunate to be working in Oxford which had escaped the bombing, although Luftwaffe aircraft flying towards the manufacturing cities in the Midlands had been a regular sight.

'One at a time!' she called then frowned as she saw a tall boy incongruously dressed in short grey trousers aim a kick at Jimmy Brown.

'Sidney! Stop that at once!'

'Tell her I ain't done nothing.' Sidney glared menacingly at the smaller boy.

He winced in pain then whispered, 'I slipped Miss Armstrong.'

She looked from one to the other and then glanced out of the window at the darkening sky. She had a long cycle ride to her rented rooms the other side of Oxford and she wanted to get home before the blackout.

'All right. But be more careful in future.'

'Yes Miss Armstrong,' whispered Jimmy.

Sidney grinned and elbowed his way out of the door.

Jimmy hung back then made his way to the cloakroom. His younger brother, Duggie, was struggling to do up the buttons of his hand-me-down overcoat.

'I got a gold star today,' he said proudly as he wound a knitted blue muffler round his neck.

'Well done!' Jimmy put on his coat and cap, slung the box containing his gas mask across his shoulder and smiled at his brother.

'I'm going to write and tell Dad,' said Duggie as he picked up his gas mask.

'And I'll write and tell him we're looking after the allotment. Mum asked us to bring a cabbage and some leeks today.'

'Can we go to the Rec first?' asked Duggie as they surged out of the school gate with the other children.

'We mustn't be long.'

Jimmy ran past some girls from his class flying high on the swings to where Duggie and another boy were beginning to push the roundabout.

'Jump on!' cried Jimmy. 'I'll make it go really fast!'

He was joined by a couple of others. They each grabbed a hand rail and went round and round until they were dizzy.

'More!' screamed the smaller boys.

Jimmy shook his head. 'We must go to the allotment.'

'There's not much left,' said Duggie as they reached their small patch of ground, one of the many allotted by the council for growing vegetables.

'No.' Jimmy frowned. 'I thought we had a cabbage.'

'I'm fed up with cabbage. Let's pull up some leeks.' Duggie grabbed the top of the nearest leek.

'That's not how to do it. You must pull from the bottom.' Jimmy bent down and eased a large leek out of the ground.

'Pow!' shouted Duggie and waved the leek in the air.

Jimmy stood up, then ducked suddenly as a cabbage came whizzing past his head. His stomach lurched as he saw Sidney and his accomplice coming towards them singing 'Run rabbit - run rabbit - Run! Run! Run!'

He grabbed Duggie's hand and they ran out of the allotments and up Aldridge Road where blackout curtains were already drawn in the council houses on either side of the road.

'That's our road,' cried Duggie as Jimmy propelled them past Buckler Road.

'I don't want them to follow us to our house.'

'But we'll crash into the wall,' wailed Duggie.

Ahead of them was a seven foot brick wall with iron spikes on the top.

Behind them the footsteps came closer.

Jimmy's heart was thumping as he realised the only way out was to hide in one of the gardens. Still holding his brother's hand he veered towards the last house but tripped and they both staggered forward straight towards the wall.

Duggie let out a piercing scream and then there was silence.

'Where are we?' Duggie tightened his grip on his brother's hand.

Jimmy stared at the large white-walled house next to them. Instead of flower beds in the front garden there was a car parked on a gravelled drive. A string of coloured lights hung above the porch.

'I think it's Wentworth Road where the posh people live.'

'It must be nice to be posh and not have to bother with the blackout.' Duggie pointed to the brightly lit houses on either side of the street.

Jimmy pricked up his ears as Christmas music sounded faintly in the distance and felt a surge of excitement. Their miraculous escape from Sidney and his friend had given him confidence.

'Come on! Let's see how the posh people live!'

Both boys broke into a run, stopping occasionally to gasp at Christmas lights twinkling inside the windows.

'Summertown's down there,' said Jimmy when they reached the end of the street.

They hurried down Banbury Road towards the music.

Everything seemed brighter as they got nearer the centre of Summertown.

In front of them a woman dressed in a bright yellow jacket was jogging next to a little girl on a scooter wearing a red hat with a light that flashed on and off.

All the shops were brightly lit and there were coloured lights in some of the trees.

Duggie looked around in amazement as they paused to listen to a brass band playing outside a shop with pictures of houses for sale in the window.

'Do you think the war has ended?' he asked.

'I don't know. It might have!'

Jimmy grabbed his brother's hand and they pushed their way towards people standing round a tall fir tree.

A silver-haired lady wearing an ornate gold chain over her coat stepped forward. 'I declare Christmas in Summertown has officially begun. The shops will remain open till 10 o'clock and the Co-op has kindly provided free mince pies,' she announced to the cheering crowd.

Suddenly the tree was lit with hundreds of lights and there was a cheer of approval from the onlookers.

'Did the lady say the mince pies are free?' Jimmy felt in his pockets but, apart from a handkerchief, they were empty.

'That's right,' answered an elderly man. 'You'd better hurry before they're all gone.' His eyes twinkled then looked puzzled as he caught sight of the box slung over Jimmy's shoulder.

'Excuse me asking, but is that a gas mask in your box?'

'Yes, Sir.' Jimmy stared at the man and fiddled with the

strap. He was getting tired of having to carry it everywhere.

Duggie tugged his brother's sleeve. 'The mince pies are over there!'

'You'd better be off then,' the man smiled at the boys as they hurried away.

They paused by a group of children wearing red pixie hats and singing a familiar Christmas song.

Tapping their feet to the music, the boys joined in the chorus:

> *'Jingle bells, jingle bells, jingle all the way.*
> *Oh! what fun it is to ride in a one-horse open sleigh.'*

'We sing that song at school,' whispered Duggie.

Jimmy nodded, unaccountably reassured by the song's familiarity.

At the end they joined the applause then walked over to a woman holding a basket of mince pies. Duggie's eyes widened as he took two.

'One each'. The woman smiled but her tone was firm.

'Please,' Duggie pleaded, 'Can I take one for my Dad?'

'Is he with you?'

'No, he's serving his country.'

The woman looked sympathetically at the two strangely dressed boys. 'I'll wrap one up for you.' She pulled a see-through bag from her pocket and popped the mince pie inside.

'We can post it to him,' said Duggie putting the bag in his pocket then taking a large bite of the mince pie he was holding.

'He'd like that,' said Jimmy doubtfully. Mention of his father made him think of their mother waiting at home.

'We must go now.' His euphoria was suddenly gone.

'But what about Sidney?' Duggie looked around fearfully.

'They'll have gone by now. We've been here ages.' Jimmy

replied with more confidence than he felt.

They looked round, wide-eyed, as they began to retrace their steps.

'I wonder if that shop belongs to the King.' Jimmy pointed to a sign saying Majestic over a shop with brightly coloured bottles in the window, some of them a rich gold colour.

Duggie pressed his nose to the window. 'I'm thirsty. Do you think they sell Tizer?'

'We haven't any money.' Both boys looked hopefully at the pavement, remembering the time they had found sixpence, but there were no coins to be seen.

'Have you lost something?' asked a familiar voice.

Smiling down at them was the elderly man who had commented on their gas masks.

'No, Sir. We were just looking for lost coins.' Jimmy straightened up. 'But we have to go now.'

The man put his hand in his coat pocket and pulled out a packet of liquorice allsorts. 'Would you like these? I won them in the tombola but I'm not particularly partial to them myself.'

'Sweets!' shouted Duggie excitedly.

Jimmy hesitated for a second then held out his hand. 'Thank you, Sir.'

He carefully opened the packet and offered it to his brother. Duggie peered inside before selecting a yellow and black sweet and popped it in his mouth.

Frowning in concentration, Jimmy selected a square shaped black and white sweet.

'Don't eat them all at once,' said the man.

'We'll make them last,' Jimmy replied earnestly as he put the packet in his pocket.

The elderly man looked at them quizzically. 'Good bye. Look after yourselves,' he said then turned and walked slowly away.

'Goodbye.' The boys replied politely.

They began to run across a small side road next to the shop with the coloured bottles.

'Watch out kids!' a blonde-haired young woman on a bicycle shouted as she swerved to avoid the boys.

'That was a near miss!' Jimmy looked admiringly at the woman peddling furiously on a purple coloured bicycle.

'Wow! A purple bike!' cried Duggie.

'Maybe she delivers important messages,' said Jimmy knowingly.

They caught up with her as she dismounted next to a table displaying a poster saying Help for Heroes. She lent her bike against some railings and took a red and white collecting tin from her saddle bag.

'People have been very generous,' she said handing the tin to a man sitting behind the table.

As he took the tin Jimmy noticed an eagle tattoo on the man's arm.

'They've been generous here too. Our furry friend has been busy this evening.' He pointed to a large teddy bear with one arm in a sling and a collecting tin between its paws.

Duggie gently stroked the bear but Jimmy looked closely at the poster showing a silhouette of a wounded man being carried on a stretcher by two soldiers.

'Our father's a hero,' he said.

'I'm sure he is.' The man with the eagle tattoo frowned slightly as he looked at the boys.

'Is your mother with you?' asked the woman encouragingly.

'She's at home getting the tea.'

'Does she know you're here?' the woman persisted.

Jimmy looked at the man who, in some way, reminded him of his father.

'We ran into a spot of bother on our way home from school,' he said airily.

'I'm not surprised,' murmured the woman as she took in the children's quaint appearance.

'Where did you get your gas masks?' the man with the tattoo asked suddenly.

Jimmy looked puzzled. 'School. Everyone's got one.'

'I expect they're doing a project on the war,' said the woman.

'That sounds like a logical explanation,' said the man. He leant forward and held out his hand, first to Jimmy and then to Duggie.

'It's been nice meeting you. Go carefully.'

'I'm sorry we haven't anything to put in the collection box,' said Jimmy.

'No worries. Generosity of spirit is the most important thing. The world would be a better place if there was more generosity.' He looked at the young woman and smiled.

'Have you got far to go?' asked the young woman.

'Cutteslowe.'

'So you don't have any busy roads to cross.'

'No.' Jimmy's heart began to beat faster as he remembered the wall. 'Let's go,' he said and began to run.

'Wait for me!' said Duggie anxiously.

When Jimmy turned to wait for his brother he saw that the man was sitting in a wheelchair.

Both boys seemed to have forgotten that they were too old to hold hands as they ran up Banbury Road together. They paused for breath when they reached Wentworth Road. They could see easily because the street lights were on and Christmas lights shone in some of the windows.

Jimmy looked ahead but was unable to make out the wall. He felt his heart pounding. Then he thought of his father and the man in the wheelchair and all the other heroes.

He squeezed Duggie's hand. 'We're nearly home. Let's walk the rest of the way.'

As they walked, Jimmy's mind was racing as he worked out what to do. When they reached the wall they would have to creep into the garden of the posh house next to the wall and hope that no one saw them. Then they had to find a way to climb out of the posh person's garden and into the council house garden nearest to it. He hoped there weren't any dogs. All would be lost if there was barking. And, in any case, Duggie was frightened of dogs.

Jimmy was so lost in thought that he didn't notice the sudden darkness. Then two white faces loomed in front of them. It was Sidney and his friend and they looked terrified.

'How did you do that?' croaked Sidney.

'Do what?' Jimmy turned. Immediately behind them was the seven foot wall.

'We went to see the Christmas lights,' said Duggie excitedly.

'Don't lie.' Sidney was beginning to return to his cocky self. 'Lights aren't allowed.'

'And anyway you've only been gone a minute,' his friend piped up.

Jimmy's head began to spin as images of the things they had seen flashed through his mind. What was it the man in the wheelchair had said?

'The world would be a better place if there was more generosity.'

He took the packet of liquorice allsorts from his pocket, opened it and offered it to the bigger boys.

Sidney went to grab the packet then hesitated and carefully took out a sweet.

'Take two,' said Jimmy calmly.

'Ta! Thanks.' He looked at Jimmy with something like respect as he selected another sweet.

Still holding the packet, Jimmy offered the sweets to the other boy and then to Duggie.

The four boys stood and munched in silence.

Then Sidney scrabbled inside his gas mask box and brought out a cabbage. It was small and worse for wear but Jimmy recognised it as the one they had dodged in the allotment; it seemed like hours ago.

'Mum will be pleased,' he said. 'It was our last one.'

Sidney nodded. 'Time to go,' he said abruptly.

With his friend following, Sidney began to walk away. Suddenly he turned, saluted and disappeared into the darkness.

Historical Notes

In 1933, Oxford City Council built the Cutteslowe housing estate to the north of the city. The following year, the Urban Housing Company bought the land between the Council Estate and Banbury Road. The developer decided that these houses could be sold at a higher price if they were separated from the council houses. In 1934 he built walls across two roads that ran through both estates in order to block off the council estate from the private houses. The walls were seven feet high and had rotating iron spikes on top. There were several attempts to remove the walls but it was not until 9th March 1959, after the city had purchased the strips of land on which the walls stood, that they were demolished.

There is a blue plaque on the house in Aldridge Road where it joins Wentworth Road to commemorate the demolition of the wall there.

There was an infants school for children aged 5-7 in Wren Road, where the current Cutteslowe primary school is. For the purpose of this story I imagine that Cutteslowe school takes juniors as well as infants during the Second World War.

There was a Rec - Recreation Ground - opposite the school and allotments along a lane at the edge of the Rec.

MALACHI STILT-JACK

JOHN KITCHEN

So that was it. The world premier of Samuel Goldstein's *Concerto for Chorus and Orchestra*. It was over and Goldstein sat there in the front row of Oxford Town Hall, sweating like a pig.

He could see the conductor, Michael Davis, leaning over the podium, beckoning and mouthing for him to come onto the stage, but he couldn't move. What was it that was going on behind him? Jeers of derision, cat-calls, whistles? What little clapping there was sounded more like water spilling from an overflow pipe. He'd written in a part for an off-stage semi-chorus, and he'd directed them to inhale helium to give the voices that high ethereal sound, and someone back there was shouting, 'Let's hear it for the chipmunks!'

'Come up, Sam!' Michael mouthed again. He was exaggerating the words as though to someone who was deaf, and the man beside him gave him a shove:

'Go on mate. Do what the guy says.'

He stumbled forward, dazed, but as he approached and Michael left the podium to greet him, the audience, thinking Michael's departure was a signal that the interval had begun, started leaving; the tepid clapping there was began to falter completely and no matter what indignities Sam had already endured, he was not going to march onto a silent stage. Before the plaudits died altogether he vaulted the platform and made it to the recently vacated rostrum to cries of, 'Wow. An acrobat!'

Michael returned and lifted the composer's hand in defiance against the derision, while still more of the audience shoved off towards the bar.

It was a fiasco. All his hopes and dreams for this evening

were dashed.

The audience had frightened him from the moment he'd seen them filing through the foyer. He knew the types: the season ticket holders who'd only come because they'd paid their whack, the middle class, smartly dressed brigade, who'd come to be seen and for the Beethoven *Choral Fantasia* and the Mozart symphony in the second half, the students and the youthfully cynical who were there for some fun, whose self-perceived intellectualism he'd always dreaded, and he'd watched them all, a conglomeration of bodies that spelled potential disaster even before the first note had been sounded.

Yet, while he stood there looking at the retreating masses, he could empathise with them. Who could blame them? You could be amazed when you saw frail Stravinsky appearing on the platform after a performance of *The Rite of Spring*. That such a diminutive man could create sinews of that sort was obviously a miracle. It was the same with Brahms and Beethoven, and Schubert. Their overt finiteness gave a magic to their music; but how could you be in awe of someone like Samuel Goldstein? Samuel Goldstein was six foot ten inches in his stockinged feet. What composer worth his salt stood on the podium at six foot ten? And in every other way he failed to look the part. His greying hair shot out in all directions like a furze bush and his beard looked like the habitat for every mini-beast God had ever created. His eyes, peering wildly through gold-rimmed spectacles, had the penetration of a madman, while his gangling legs seemed to put him on stilts. It was no wonder he was being bombarded by cat-calls. He would have been more at home in a circus.

And any remains of clapping were dying while he stood there and still, in the dark confusion below him, he could see people slipping away to the bar.

In shame he turned and left the podium, bowing from the shoulders to make himself look less ungainly and before he reached the wings he could have sworn the hall had emptied completely.

There was no way he could face Michael, not after the unstinting work he had put into this travesty, nor could he face the orchestra and chorus who'd commissioned it, and blindly he rushed for the exit.

But he was unprepared for the shock of emergence, and he stood, stunned, on the steps for a moment. He had completely forgotten that it was June. Had he stumbled into the murk of November, the transition would have been easier; but, an evening in June, and such an evening, with the sun at full strength…

He must escape - get himself away from the scene of the crime. By now he'd convinced himself that it *was* a crime. If he hung around the doors of the Town Hall someone would come out in pursuit, or a member of the audience would appear and recognise his stilt legs and the metallic fuzz, and they'd start falling about laughing.

He made it, unchecked to the High Street and then he relaxed slightly. He was less conspicuous here. At last he could begin to imagine himself a normal being, lost in the milling throngs.

But the relief was short-lived. A grey drunk sidled up to him as he moved towards the Turl. His intention was to wheedle money to support his drinking habit, but as he approached Sam, he teetered on the pavement and craned his neck in disbelief. Instead of pleading for any spare change, he gasped, 'Be Jesus, would you mind telling me what the weather's like up there?' And then he shuffled off, satisfied without his coin, muttering audibly, 'It would be the frost on his beard making it look like that, no doubt.'

Sam heard him and he smiled bitterly. Normal he most certainly was not.

He was hurt though. His beloved Oxford, his own university city, had smacked him in the face. He'd only occasionally come back here since his student days and he'd quite forgotten how heady it all was. He'd had his loyal friends in those days and the avant-garde stuff he'd composed for them had made him something of a cult figure. He sighed as he wandered down the Turl and turned towards the Radcliffe Camera. The cloistered, protected world of this lovely city had duped him then. When he'd been here as a student life had stretched away full of promise and a potential for greatness - for success and… for acclaim. That was the thing he looked for most, to be acknowledged and recognised, and in those long-lost days, it had all seemed possible.

But that was fifty years ago.

A sycamore tree stood sentinel to the Radcliffe Square, and he stopped beneath it, staring. At seventy Oxford had turned on him. No longer were the students his friends and admirers. The familiar faces had grown old along with him. His tutor back in those days had been a mere five years older than he was and he'd almost been part of the gang - but, today, even he had put him down.

He'd gone to visit him this afternoon, full of the excitement of the old tutorials, but a great transformation had greeted him. Cold courtesy, a suspicion of Don for Don, a salvo delivered with the delicate, deadly charm known only to elderly university scholars.

'How lovely to see you my boy. What brings you back to Oxford? You've done something for the Pro-Musica? How perfectly commendable. Now, tell me,' settling back in his heavy leather chair, with his long white hair hanging like a lampshade around his puffy face; his eyes gleaming for the kill. 'How does it feel to be a professor yourself? Don't you find that these young things revitalise you with their youth? And how *is* Wessex, anyway? Tell me about it - being a professor in a red-brick establishment?'

He wandered across the square, past the church of St Mary the Virgin and sank onto a bench set in an alcove in All Soul's. He looked across to the Radcliffe Camera with the Bodleian standing proud behind it. It was such a perfect place, void of traffic and so tranquil and architecturally sublime, the monumental buildings and the long shadows, the innocuous warmth of the Cotswold stone.

He sighed. He'd wanted a meteoric ascent to fame and glory but he'd reached seventy and all he'd achieved was, a few works for local village festivals, a children's opera and a *Concerto Grosso* for the Proms. A *Concerto Grosso*! He'd wanted to shake the world and the only commission that had given him the least chance of recognition was an ephemeral little neoclassical piece for a late-night Prom. There wasn't another composer he could name who'd achieved so little. He shook his head and watched as a disorderly line of boys rambled across the square, anxiously pursued by their master. The only meteoric ascent Sam was likely to experience, he thought, was when he stood up.

The forward guard of rampaging youths seemed to be of the same opinion. He could hear fragments of their comments as they nudged each other, glancing in his direction. 'The guy on that seat - Daddy long-legs… he's got his knees hung around his ears, look… Must be some sort of a giant… where would you get trousers to fit that?'

'Boys, boys!' The master pushed and buffeted his charges like a hyperactive shunting engine. 'Such rudeness, whispering and giggling like that.' He hustled them into the semblance of a group and marched them towards the gate of St Mary's Church, nodding half apologetically in Sam's direction. They were wanting the tower. It was closed of course and the groans followed by the abject apology from the master did not surprise Sam. Nor did it surprise him when the master went in search of the Brass Rubbing Centre which had vacated the vaults in favour of a restaurant thirty years earlier.

The boys exploded across the path and out onto the quad and Sam watched as the little man struggled to regain control. One of his flock had gone AWOL. 'Braithwaite,' he heard him cry. 'Where is Braithwaite? Oh why does he have to be so difficult. Was he with us when we got here, boys?'

Sam could see the miscreant. He'd climbed the perimeter fence of the church and was secreted behind some shrubs by the vault.

Uncoiling himself from his seat in the alcove, he arose.

'I think it's your brat that's hiding in those bushes,' he murmured.

The wilting pedagogue simpered, struggling for restraint. 'Brat? Oh I wouldn't say brat. It's just youthful high spirits you know?' And he pranced off in the direction of the vaults.

Sam stared icily at the remaining boys and then strode off, their stifled giggles teasing his ears as he went.

It was the legs, of course. Somewhere, Yeats had written about Sam's legs. Malachi Stilt-Jack the character was called.

"I through the terrible novelty of light, stalk on, stalk on;"

A spectacle to be gawped at. A clown without dignity.

There was a rich aroma of nostalgia in the air as he progressed towards Longwall; an evocation of coffee and warm bread and with the smell he'd been thrown back again to student times, the frequent visits to those coffee houses, the rowing, the tennis and cricket, the long afternoons lounging by the river down by Angel Meadow, the hot, sunny days, the concerts… Yes! The concerts! In this unguarded moment it all came flooding back, and one concert in particular. Benjamin Britten. That had been his undoing. He would never forget it, never in his life.

It was a Prom. The first prom performance of the *War Requiem*. He'd been with Michael at that too, and how different it had been from their partnership this evening. Together they'd sat, spell-bound, as the disturbing music unfolded, the brass fanfares of the *Dies Irae*, and that unbearably moving *Lacrimosa*. Then the *In Paradisum* with its nebulous plainsong, first, the distant boys singing their hymn, then the chorus taking it up, voice after voice, until the soprano soloist came in and the whole hall seemed to tremble with indefinable heavenly music; and there was this man, stooping at the shoulders, beating out the bars with his white baton, and he was so innocuous, his brown wavy hair cropped like an office clerk, and you would have passed him on the street without a second glance, but he was a god. That bowed being had created all this sublime sound out of his own head, sound that was almost too moving to be endured, and Sam had wept. There were others too, touched beyond measure; and then the stunned silence after the last fading chord, followed by clapping such as he'd never heard before. And there he'd stood, with Fischer-Dieskau on one side, and on the other, Heather Harper, holding his hand as if he was a lost school boy. And it was then that Sam had said to himself… one day, this will happen to me.

He was by Magdalen gate now, staring at the converging perspective of the honey coloured college, tapering away towards the tower and the bridge, and there were tears in his eyes again, because, if there was a time when the impact of tonight's fiasco touched him most deeply, it was now. Where had it all gone? Those empty, intervening years?

Couples passed by, idly chatting, knots of students and tourists converging inconsequentially. By the ice cream stand behind him some boys were grouped looking at something saucy on an iPhone. They were huddled in uninhibited glee. Suddenly their laughter pealed as the one with the iPhone ran back towards Longwall Street, pursued by the others, and Sam envied them; he envied them all.

Slowly he made his way towards the bridge. That easy inter flow, creating friendship, he hadn't got that. He couldn't be easy in company. Without his music, he was nothing.

Perhaps it wasn't the best time to arrive at Magdalen Bridge.

Beneath him, on the bottle-brown waters of the Cherwell,

punters nosed under the laden trees, ducking branches and swerving from swarms of suspended gnats, while away to his right was Angel Meadow, where tourists and students would be spread out on their rugs with bottles of wine and food, watching the idle meanderings of the river.

It would be foolish to jump. Nothing but embarrassment could come of it. He could stand in that water, but contemplating such an act had an unexpected effect. Sam, you see, suffered from an affliction. At six foot ten in his stockinged feet, Sam Goldstein had vertigo. From his vantage point the drop over the bridge looked like miles, and with the length of his legs, the barrier wall seemed to be no more than a pivot to unbalance him. As he gazed down at the river, it all began to lurch and swirl. He felt his long, stilt legs crumble. His body described a drunken circle and he tumbled to the ground.

'Stand back, boys. Give the gentleman room to breathe.'

He was aware of one voice above the chatter as he came to, and he winced. It was that old pedagogue from Radcliffe Square with his unruly mob. He opened his eyes and immediately above him, like an anxious full moon, scarred with lines of premature worry, hovered the horn-rimmed glasses and the bushy eyebrows of the teacher.

'I'm so sorry,' Sam muttered.

'Braithwaite! Braithwaite,' the full moon called. The black sheep approached. 'Quickly, to the minibus and bring me the First Aid box.' He scrabbled for some keys and Braithwaite, grabbing them, hoofed it towards the St Clements car park.

'It's all right,' Sam protested. 'There's no need to bother.'

'It's no bother,' the master assured him.

Sam propped himself against the wall and the laconic youths who had previously surrounded him, disheartened that no death was imminent, drifted further down the bridge.

'I've got a little nip of whisky in the First Aid box,' the old man whispered.

Sam shook his head. 'It's all right,' he said again. He smiled. To be honest he found the concern faintly gratifying; but some explanation was called for. 'I've had an emotionally charged evening,' he said. 'I'm a composer, you see. I've just had a new work performed at the Town Hall. I expect it all got a bit too much for me.'

Beneath the bushy eyebrows, the eyes lit up. 'A composer?' the little man repeated. Then: 'Boys, boys!'

The rabble returned, hoping for a sudden deterioration in Daddy long-leg's physical state. 'Boys,' the teacher gabbled excitedly. 'This gentleman is a composer. Oh, how fortuitous.' He turned to Sam again. 'It so happens that my boys are members of a choir school. We saw the new work advertised.' His eyes twinkled with animation. 'So you're the composer?' He hesitated and then… 'I don't suppose we could prevail upon you to write something for us, for our summer festival next year?'

By now Braithwaite had returned and Sam heard one of the other boys mutter to him, 'The stilt-man writes music. Flash is nobbling him to compose something for us.'

He felt much better suddenly. After his nip of whisky and a talk with them all he made his way towards Angel Meadow.

He would sit by the river for a while and think. He remembered those early days in Oxford, and that performance of the *War Requiem*. He recalled the thrill shivering down his body as he'd listened to it, and… at times during the *Concerto for Chorus and Orchestra* he'd felt the same electrifying excitement.

Perhaps people hadn't understood it yet, but he'd certainly said something, and if there were other performances, then… who knows?

He would write a liturgical work for the boys; a *Missa Brevis*, perhaps. Yes, a *Missa Brevis*.

In the evening light, trees hung heavily over the Cherwell,

and Oxford, dear old Oxford, had duped him again.
Ideas began to formulate in his mind.

THE RADCLIFFE LEGACY

LINORA LAWRENCE

May shivered as she stood on the edge of the road in Catte Street, not surprisingly, given the date, the 1st of December 1714. She pulled her shawl more firmly around her shoulders, but she would gladly have suffered more cold than this, so determined was she to see Dr Radcliffe's coffin come past and go through the Great Gates of the Schools Quadrangle to be met by the Vice Chancellor and the Proctors of the University. The gates were, by now, open giving her a glimpse of the members of Convocation gathered, as they had been bidden, ready to escort the embalmed remains of the honoured doctor to the Divinity School. He was to lie in state like a king for two days prior to his funeral which would take place on the Friday in the Church of St Mary the Virgin in the High Street. She had come out very early to secure a good place though it meant she was not with her husband. He had said he would close his apothecary's shop only when word spread that the hearse had actually arrived in Oxford, coming as it was from the good doctor's estate at Carshalton in Surrey.

The noise from the crowd gave May ample warning that the procession was approaching. It gave her time to tear herself away from her memories and bring herself back to the present. She wanted to honour the doctor whose wise instruction, some thirty years previously, had almost certainly saved her mother's life.

She recalled that morning when, after she and her sister had nursed their mother through the most terrible night, fearing every hour that they would lose her, she had made up her mind to walk from their home in Yarnton to Oxford to try to find the doctor who it was said had cured the wife of

Sir Thomas Spencer, the 'lord' of Yarnton Manor.

'You will have to do the milking by yourself,' she instructed her little sister, Dorothy.

'Will you be back for the afternoon milking?'

'I don't know. I don't think so. It's not just the walking to Oxford; I have to find the doctor when I get there.'

'I hope you can find a cart coming back. I mean a nice one, someone kind.'

'I hope so too,' May replied and with that she left, clutching her package of bread and cheese to sustain her through her long day. It was early summer and the birds sang to her as she walked. In fact, they were her only companions for the first two miles or so. After that she saw the occasional farm hand making his way to work which reminded her of the home farm where she and her sister helped in the dairy under the watchful eye of Mistress Bale. There were always seasonal jobs requiring extra hands on a farmstead. Their mother helped out whenever required, with the one exception of milking duties. She had been kicked by a cow as a small child which left her with an abiding fear of the creatures. When harvest time came, naturally everyone pitched in and remembering last Harvest Festival and how much the men had loved her mother's fruit pies gave May a warm glow of pride.

At last she began to see familiar landmarks which told her she was nearing the city of Oxford. She passed Diamond Hall, but gave the inn a wide berth bearing in mind its reputation as a highwayman's den. Another twenty minutes walking saw her passing Wholeston's Farm where fruit and vegetables were grown for sale to the inhabitants of the city. Soon she would reach Oxford itself and she still hadn't a plan as to how find the doctor.

Out of habit May took the route her mother favoured turning left into the Broad Street passing the wide ditch that had been so filled in with rubbish over the years that some folk had risked building cottages on it. She came to Turl

Street where the twirling gate admitted her to the centre. Almost the first shop she noticed had blue and green glass bottles on display augmented with a scattering of herbs. Ah, an apothecary's thought May. They should know where the doctor lives and she ventured inside. She waited until a customer was bowed out of the door and then she asked her question. What she did not expect was the explosion of an answer. 'I would not advise you where to find that man if he was the last doctor in Oxford! He doesn't know one medication from another. He's a charlatan, a disgrace to his profession!' A young apprentice cowered in the corner as his master continued his rant. May made her apologies and left feeling quite shaken. As chance would have it the previous customer had forgotten one of his purchases and the apprentice was sent out to run after him. He caught up with May. 'Don't take on,' he said seeing tears threatening to fall. 'Master Green, he hates that Dr Radcliffe because he does not send his patients to us to buy our potions. In fact they had a big argument about one of our mixtures. He said it was doing the patients more harm than good. I can tell you where to find the doctor. He lodges in Lincoln College - just here.' He pointed at vast, wooden gates ahead. Clearly in a great hurry the boy ran on leaving May to screw up her courage and ask the porter for Dr Radcliffe.

'And who might you be, young miss, asking for the likes of Dr Radcliffe?'

'My name is May Woolland and I wish to consult the doctor.' Her reply engendered only more sarcasm. 'Oh, you wish to consult the good doctor, do you? You have the means to pay him for this consultation I presume?' The porter looked May up and down and sniffed loudly which clearly indicated, 'No, I thought not.' This interchange may have gone on for some time, but for a rude interruption in the form of two gentlemen appearing from the diagonally opposite corner of the quadrangle, heading towards the porters' lodge and arguing loudly with each other.

'Dr Radcliffe, give me one good reason why the college should alter its statutes just to accommodate you,' said the older man, in a raised voice.

'Oh, my law it's the Rector,' gasped the porter. 'Good morning Rector, I mean, my Lord, my Lord Bishop, ohhh, I mean…'

'For goodness sakes, man, I may be the Bishop of Oxford,' exclaimed an exasperated Lord Crewe, but I am still the Rector of this College and you may continue to address me as Rector in this context. How many times have we had this conversation?'

Radcliffe's eyes suddenly sparkled, 'My Lord, may I appeal to you in your capacity as Bishop of this diocese?'

'No, you may not,' retorted Crewe. 'I would not dream of overruling the Rector of Lincoln College. Now, my duties call me. We must continue this conversation on another occasion if there is anything more to say, that is.'

'In that case, I wish you a very good morrow, my Lord,' replied Radcliffe sweeping a bow. The porter was by this time sitting down and wiping the sweat from his wide forehead. He was in even more awe of Lincoln College's Head of House since he had, in an unprecedented move, been made Bishop of the newly created Diocese of Oxford.

'Please sir, are you Dr Radcliffe, sir?' May asked.

'I am indeed that same person. How may I assist you my child?' The doctor's humour had clearly undergone a major change in a positive direction.

May's story tumbled out. She described her mother's condition, the tremendously high fever and now the numerous red spots appearing all over her body. The porter, listening to this, was showing signs of becoming hysterical. 'The pox, the pox,' he cried out, 'Get her out of here!' He would have seized May by the shoulders and pushed her out on to the street except that he didn't want to touch her.

'You, stupid man,' said Radcliffe, 'I shall remove her from your presence since you seem to think you are at great personal risk. Indeed, perhaps you are,' he added cryptically. 'Come child,' he indicated that May should follow him. 'That man will be the death of me, if I don't bring about his demise first.' He still seemed cheerful May thought. Perhaps he liked these verbal fights. She knew two men on the farm who were like that with each other.

She followed the doctor through a door, up a flight of stairs and into his set of rooms where she gazed around. A skeleton was hung in one corner which made her shiver. A few vials stood on his desk and a herbal lay open showing an illustration which gave her a clue as to the volume's contents. She would have expected many more learned volumes to be lying around, or rather when she thought about it afterwards and described her visit to others.

'Come, tell me how you have been looking after your mother,' said Radcliffe. May responded describing how she and her sister had followed Mistress Bale's instructions: keeping all windows shut so that none of that dangerous outside air could get in, keeping her wrapped up as warmly as possible, trying to make her drink milk like a baby.

'Now,' said Radcliffe, apparently changing the subject, 'You say your name is May, but I think me, that cannot be your baptismal name?'

'No sir, I was baptised Millicent in Saint Bartholomew's church in Yarnton. My mother says I am called May because the may blossom was coming out when I was born.'

Radcliffe's face lit up, 'Ah, one of my sisters is named Millicent. An excellent choice, if I may say so. Yarnton, ah yes, I remember Yarnton. Now, how came you to this fair city to find me?'

'Please, sir, I walked, sir.' There was a tremble in May's voice.

'Sit you down, child. If I am not much mistaken you

are clutching your victuals. Eat them before you faint away before me. You will not be able to help your mother if you do not keep up your own strength.' May sat down gratefully and, after some hesitation, unfolded her cloth.

'Now, Miss May, listen to me while you eat. I will tell you what you can do to give your mother her best chance of recovery. But, you will be surprised at what you are going to hear. Do you trust me, Miss May? Will you do what I say?' His voice had changed and was serious now.

'Yes, sir, I will, sir. I do trust you, with all my heart!'

Radcliffe smiled. 'Keep eating, child. You will the better remember my advice if you have food in your stomach.' He proceeded to instruct May to open the windows and clean everything in the bedroom to the best of her ability. 'Do you have a good supply of fresh water?' he asked. The reply was that the farm had two wells which Radcliffe was pleased to hear. 'Wash your mother down as often as possible, perhaps twice a day. Keep bathing her wrists and her forehead and the back of her knees,' he added. 'Wash her bedding so that she is not lying in her own sweat and worse.' He proceeded to warn May that the spots would get worse but that as they did, the fever itself would lessen. 'They will burst and scabs will form,' the doctor continued, 'Let them dry and try to stop your mother scratching them. As to eating, do not give her milk until the fever is quite gone. If she can take anything at all a little broth would be good. Most importantly, get her to drink as much water as she possibly can.' He asked May to repeat the instructions back to him which she did.

'Tell, me child, if there had been a medicine I could have recommended, how would you have proposed to pay for it?'

May looked anxious but she had her reply ready. 'I thought, sir that I could work for you, sir. I have no money to pay for anything. We all work on the farm not for money, but for food and to live in our cottage. I thought I could work in your kitchen, sir and I can cook. I can bake an apple pie near as good as my mother's.' As she thought of her mother the tears, once more, threatened to spill.

'Well, you have thought it all out,' exclaimed Radcliffe. 'I like that, but you could not know that I am a Fellow of this college and I dine in the Great Hall every evening. I have no need of a maid.'

May looked at him anxiously. 'However, that may change,' he mused, as much to himself as to May. 'Yes, indeed, that may have to change.' After a long pause, he announced firmly, 'I will make a bargain with you Miss May. If I move out of this college and have need of a maid I will send for you at the Home Farm at Yarnton and, if you are not yet wed, then I will expect you to come into my service.' He beamed at May and she gave him her widest smile back. 'Come, you must start your journey home. I will walk with you to the Cornmarket and we shall see if a carter is going towards Woodstock.'

Clip clop went the horses' hooves - the cortege was approaching. 'I could never have imagined how great it would be,' May told her family afterwards. 'Six grey horses pulled the funeral carriage, but before that came twenty white horses leading the way. I counted ten pages dressed in mourning and then six carriages with grand folk in them following behind.' There had been quite a to-do when it came to turning into Catte Street, she related. What with the crowds and the twenty ridden horses there was no room for the carriages to turn around. In the end someone had taken charge and ordered that they should come one at a time to the Great Gates, allowing the occupants to alight before turning and making their way back to the Broad Street.

It was the talk of the town. Taverns were full of folk discussing Wednesday's events. It was said that every Master of Arts was presented with a gold mourning ring and a pair of mourning gloves.' 'That will cost a pretty penny,' folks were saying to each other, 'given that there are 300 of them!' However, the lavish funeral arrangements came as no great surprise as it had already become generally known, probably due to the Master of University College, Radcliffe's great friend Arthur Charlett, who was an incorrigible gossip, that Dr Radcliffe had not long since made what was to be his final Will and had left a great legacy to the University.

'Truly we are living in times of great change what with our good Queen Anne dying in the summer and now Dr Radcliffe in November. Whatever will happen next?' asked Daniel the apothecary, May's husband.

May was wondering if there was any possibility of viewing her erstwhile employer laid out in the Divinity School. She was not one of the great and the good, but she had worked in the Doctor's employment when he had left Lincoln College and set himself up in his own lodgings in Oxford. Radcliffe had remembered his promise and sent for May to come and be his maid determined as he was to surround himself with a happy and comfortable household though, it must be said, he was as likely to be found sharing a drink and some gossip in the local taverns as to be entertaining at home. He had finally parted company with Lincoln as the College's statutes stated that all Fellows must eventually take holy orders regardless of whatever other subjects they had studied. While a pious man, Radcliffe had no inclination to study anything that did not relate to medicine. Besides, his reputation had spread and he was earning a respectable living.

Daniel, knowing how much it meant to May, asked around and was eventually able to speak with one of the proctors. It was arranged that May and her husband could pay their respects at six o'clock in the evening of the Thursday. May was very quiet as she and Daniel walked down Brasenose Lane, the back route to the Divinity School. She wasn't at all sure how she would feel and yet she knew she would deeply regret it if she did not take this opportunity to say goodbye. She tried to count the years since she had last seen the doctor. He had moved to London and she had married Daniel, the apothecary's young apprentice, borne his children and learned to be a good wife. However, Dr Radcliffe had made many visits back to Oxford to see friends and had called into the Pharmacy to congratulate them on the birth of their first child or to ask if another baby was on the way or had, indeed, arrived. Daniel had drunk a cup of coffee with the good doctor more than once in the Angel Coffee House in the High Street.

With trepidation, they entered the Divinity School, surely one of the most beautiful stone rooms in Europe. Its exquisite Gothic carvings never ceased to amaze the onlooker, but today everything was draped in black cloth. There were dozens of escutcheons. The coffin was surrounded by a rail covered in velvet, with twelve silver candlesticks and plumes of black and white feathers.

Daniel paused to speak to one of the ushers. May, in the meantime, approached the dais and gently touched the elm wood casket. She couldn't form a proper sentence to say goodbye, so she did the one thing she could do for the doctor now - she whispered the Lord's Prayer and asked God to take him straight to heaven remembering all the people whose lives he had saved and whose illnesses he had cured. 'And please forgive him for offending others,' she added, 'mostly other doctors, but You will know that.'

Daniel moved towards her, touched her elbow and smiled at her gently, a smile which said, 'Are you all right?' May nodded, smiled back and whispered, 'Thank you,' and after a little while they moved away, circling the rail as they did so. After one last backward glance, they left the room knowing they would never forget those very special minutes.

Back in the fresh air as they walked home in the dark, Daniel, seeking to lift his wife's spirits, asked, 'What is your greatest memory of the doctor, apart from saving your mother's life, of course. I mean, what do you remember best from when you worked for him before we were married?'

'Oh,' May replied, pausing for thought, 'I think it was all the interesting people I met coming to his lodgings. There were his patients consulting him, of course, but I mean his friends and acquaintances. I did like that Mr Evelyn. He had such lovely manners. Then there was that Mr Aubrey, he was a strange one! I remember he used to talk about stone circles and such like. I wasn't too sure about all that.'

'And there were some doctors he respected, weren't there?' Daniel prompted.

'Oh, yes, certainly there were some he truly admired. There was Mr Sydenham and Mr Willis.' By this time May was positively chatting. 'He had all their books, though he told folks he didn't read medical books, but I know he did trust in theirs.'

'He never wrote any books himself, did he?' remarked Daniel.

'No, he was a 'doing' sort of a person,' replied May. 'And a talking sort of a person. He really enjoyed debating with that clever Mr Hooke - the moon and the stars man, I called him. You know who I mean.' May squeezed her husband's hand and he knew she was now feeling more cheerful. 'The things we used to overhear, when the doctor had guests and we were serving the food - we didn't understand half the time what they were on about, but it got us thinking!' After a moment's reflection, May returned to her husband's original question. 'I think my best memory is of us servants telling stories by the fire in the kitchen. It was always after we had served dinner to the doctor and his guests if he was entertaining. After we had cleared up and everything was washed and done we would sit there while the fire died down for the night, and take it in turns to tell stories. It could be just something that had happened through the day or some gossip from the market stalls or a passing traveller.'

They reached the front door of their home and before lifting the latch and entering, May paused and looked up at the moon. 'It will be a sadder world without Dr Radcliffe in it,' she said wistfully.

'His legacy will live on,' Daniel replied. 'I don't mean just his fortune; I mean all his learning and the good he did. A lot of people have learnt from that and his good practices will live on, I'm sure of it.'

Comforted by her husband's wise words May smiled and nodded in agreement. They opened the door and stepped in to their home where they were greeted by their children eager to hear how they had fared during the past hour, a tale which was to be repeated often in the days to come.

Historical Notes

John Radcliffe was born in Wakefield, Yorkshire in either 1650 or 1652. He was never sure of his precise age and there is some evidence to suggest that though a baby was born to his parents and baptised John in 1650, it died in infancy to be followed in due course by the birth of a healthy male child which was given the same name, a common practice in those days.

When he died on 1st November 1714 he left an estate of £140,000, a veritable fortune in the early 18th century. He provided handsomely for his two sisters, Hannah and Millicent, his nephews and his servants. He also made some individual bequests but the major beneficiary was the University of Oxford with £40,000 earmarked for the building of a library, plus provision for the purchase of books and the annual salary of a librarian. This was to be the Radcliffe Camera. One individual bequest worth noting was the provision of £500 a year to St Bartholomew's Hospital 'towards mending their diet' and £100 'for buying Linen.'

The charitable trust founded by his will of 13 September 1714 still operates today.

Further Reading

S. Hebron, Dr Radcliffe's Library, Bodleian Library, Oxford 2014.

D. Cranston, John Radcliffe and his Legacy to Oxford, Words by Design, Bicester, 2013.

THE DAY THE SNOW FELL

BEN McSEOIN

The day the snow fell was the day Vita murdered her mother.

Muriel was confined to her sickbed, in the living room. The curtains were open, exposing the endlessly falling snowflakes. Muriel didn't register her daughter's entrance into the room. She was too engrossed in her daily Sudoku. She didn't even flinch as Vita pretended to adjust her pillows. It was only as Vita forced one of them over her face that Muriel reacted. She tried to put up a fight, but at eighty-four, and recovering from a minor stroke, she was too feeble and soon accepted her fate.

Once the deed was done, Vita stepped back and stared down at her mother, slumped against the headrest, her eyes staring lifelessly at the ceiling. A moment passed and Vita drew the curtains, quietly leaving the room, pulling the door behind her.

Standing in the narrow hallway, she luxuriated in this sudden feeling of silence. Absolute silence. The feeling of finally being alone.

A gust of winter seeped its way through the keyhole and sent a shiver of excitement through her. I think I'll build a snowman, she thought to herself, and reached for her dark cloak hanging on the wall.

Osney Island always looked beautiful, but particularly stunning in the snow. The road was safely gritted and the pavements were neatly shovelled, but the snow continued to fall, like confetti, and the surrounding green trees were caked in it. Vita took a deep breath, digesting the crisp air, and slowly she made her way along Swan Street and over the little wooden bridge that led her out of the island.

The children in the local primary school were playing outside, their parents having dropped them off for the day. Vita looked at them, relishing life, and for a moment she smiled, before the painful memories returned…

'Can I go to that school, Mummy?'

'No.'

'Why? We live just around the corner?'

'Precisely. I don't want those little monsters knowing where we live.'

And that was why Muriel chose Saint Francis Middle School in North Oxford for her daughter.

It could have been a nice school. But it was a little too far to walk and the children thought she was weird - she wasn't allowed to watch TV, she didn't know who Patrick Swayze was and they mocked the way she always came into school wearing old lady shoes, long skirts and with her hair in tight pigtails.

'No! Please, Mummy - I look silly!'

'You look presentable.'

'But everyone laughs at me!'

'Ha! Common little upstarts.'

By now Vita had reached the West Oxford recreation ground. It was glistening in white. Thank goodness I brought my sunglasses, she thought to herself. Inspecting the site more closely, she could see all the footprints from the early morning snowman makers.

'Monsters,' she hissed and continued on her journey along the path beside the field, over the bridge and into the field beyond. There were traces of humans in the snow here too and Vita knew that this wasn't appropriate either. She'd have to pursue her journey further.

It all began when Vita was eight.

Until then, she, Muriel and her father had lived a life of eminence in a North Oxford mansion, seldom even leaving

Norham Gardens. Ernest Hermann was a professor in astrophysics at Divinity College, as was his wife who retained minor fame in Oxford as one of the college's first female alumni. Vita was a 'late baby', as Muriel once described her, born long after both her parents had turned forty, and she was educated at Fawns Preparatory School.

But then, when Vita was eight, Ernest abruptly abandoned his wife for his secretary. A divorce soon followed, with the house being sold and Muriel and Vita being forced to take up refuge elsewhere. Vita's prospects of a place at Oxford Ladies College melted away and she was hastily enrolled at Saint Francis the following term. As for a house, mother and daughter settled on Osney Island as it was far enough away from Norham Gardens, thus affordable, but still accessible to North Oxford. The day they left Norham Gardens was the day Vita last saw her father.

'He's dead, Vita. Say it.'
'My father is dead.'
'He died the day he left us for that slut.'
'He died the day he left us for that slut.'
'Mean it.'
'He died the day he left us for that slut!'
'And don't you ever forget it.'

By the time Vita reached the entrance to Willow Walk, she was forced to stop for a moment to catch her breath. Bullstake Stream to her left was frozen over, the snow landing delicately on the surface of the ice. To her right on the horizon, barely visible, was Seacourt Tower, its puny little spire trying in vain to fight the blizzard. The surrounding trees stubbornly clenched the snow; the path was drowning in it. Vita pretended she was Lucy in *The Lion, The Witch and The Wardrobe* and imagined that, at any moment now, a chariot pulled by horses would come along with Jadis, the

White Witch, sitting inside. Vita tried to smile at the thought but as she imagined Jadis tilting her head towards her, all she saw was Muriel glaring menacingly at her. With her red and angry face, she looked more like The Queen of Hearts than The White Witch.

Vita shook away the thought and continued on her journey, through North Hinksey, under the abnormally quiet A34 and then taking the far left up towards Westminster College. The snow continued to fall. Once she reached the top of the hill, she made her way along the jagged bushy lane, eventually opening up onto an Arctic wilderness. She turned and could just see, glistening in the distance, Oxford's snow covered spires. She exhaled in joy and watched her breath being carried by the icy breezes.

It was slightly further along on the grassy mounds leading up onto Cumnor Hurst that Vita decided to build her snowman. She knew the area so well and she knew how secluded it was from the rest of the world. She'd come up here a lot during her adolescent years. It was only a stone's throw from Cumnor Rise Comprehensive School where poor Vita had been forced to spend her final four years of education. Osney Island was just outside Thameside Upper School's catchment area, where most Saint Francis pupils went. During Physical Education, lunch times and all other suitable times of the day, Vita would be found up here, amongst the trees, watching the birds, collecting conkers, anything as long as she was away from those horrible pupils who made her school life a living hell.

Scraping the snow into a wide pile, Vita continued building and building until the Snowman was as tall as she was. Then it was time for the arms. Using a pair of fallen branches, she stuck them into either side of his torso. Then she looked at him, smiled and named him Joshua… Joshua… J…o…s…h…u…a

After the one boy at Cumnor Rise who had dared glance

at her more than once.

The boy who nicknamed her Veetie.

The boy who accepted her invitation round to tea at her house after school.

The boy who had been utterly humiliated by her mother.

'Veetie?'

'Yeah.'

'Ah aha - it's Vi-ta.'

Muriel's extra emphasis on the two syllables still echoed their way across Vita's mind. Without even needing to close her eyes, she could see the look of discomfort on poor Joshua's face and the way he shuffled awkwardly, as teenagers do.

'It's just a nickname... just a bit of fun.'

And then the image of Muriel and her mocking smile...

'Maybe so, young man, but I'd prefer it if you didn't. I don't suppose you've heard of Vita Sackville-West, have you?'

'... No. No, I haven't.'

'Well, when you get yourself a place at Oxford, look her up in any book at the Bodleian. You'll be blown away.'

And as Muriel finished her sentence, she winked at Joshua. It was the only time Vita ever recalled her mother doing such a thing and that made it all the more horrible.

It was her own fault, Vita acknowledged, she should have scolded Muriel then and there for daring to humiliate her first house guest. But she hadn't. She'd just stood there, blankly, watching in defeat as Joshua discreetly made his apologies and left the house, only addressing Vita again at school when he joined in all the taunts and insults hurled at her from the rest of their school peers.

'You resent me, don't you, Vita?'

'What, Mummy?'

'The way I spoke to that boy, all those years ago... I did it for you, darling, you know that, don't you?'

'... Yes, Mummy.'

'They always let you down in the end, boys. Always. Look

at your father.'

'I know, Mummy.'

'Do you?'

'... Yes, Mummy.'

'Say it.'

'Boys always let you down... in the end... just like my father.'

'... Mean it.'

'Boys always let you down in the end. Just like my father.'

'Good girl.'

Vita blocked out the painful memories and looked back at her new Joshua standing gracefully on the hill. She smiled and imagined that he would come to life, taking her by the hands, and waltzing around the hill to the tune of Tchaikovsky's *The Nutcracker*, while everyone else - dog-walkers, birdwatchers, snooty academics, those monsters at Cumnor Rise who made her life a misery, would stand by and watch in envy. And then, when the sun inevitably returned, Vita and Joshua would melt away together, leaving nothing but a trickle of icy residue.

Vita looked at Joshua and realised he was missing something. Clothes, a hat, eyes! She laughed at her silliness and, promising him she would return, quickly hurried away.

Upon her return to Osney Island, she saw Arnold standing outside the house, knocking at the front door. He was an inquisitive fool, one of Muriel's former pupils who insisted on meeting her regularly at *The Old Parsonage* for afternoon tea. Nosey. Interfering. Precocious. He was around the same age as Vita but spoke and dressed far beyond his age. She paced up to him and he turned and smiled, overly friendly.

'Ah, Vita, gosh, you're bright red... are you all right?'

'What do you want?'

'... I decided to walk home. The city centre's gridlocked,' he replied before adding, 'I wondered if your mother was up to visitors?'

The Day the Snow Fell

'Not at the moment.'

'Oh, that's a pity. Perhaps I'll call back tomorrow.' He smiled and proceeded to walk away. Vita stood watching him, admiring his suede cap, his matching jacket and auburn-coloured scarf. After a moment, she called after him. He turned and looked at her.

'On second thoughts,' she smiled, 'why don't you come in? I'm sure my mother would love to see you.'

Arnold graciously accepted and retraced his footsteps, eagerly following Vita into the house and down the corridor towards Muriel's resting place.

When Vita returned to the Hurst, she could see Joshua still standing grandly atop the hill. But there was a group of people with him. Three girls. Three teenage girls, no doubt bunking off from school.

'OI!' she screamed. They turned and looked at her, 'GET AWAY FROM HIM!'

The girls stared at her, undeterred. Vita pushed her way through the metal gate and stormed up the hill towards them. They continued glaring at her, their ragged school fleeces identifying them as contemporary pupils at Cumnor Rise.

'Get away from him!' Vita hissed again.

The Girl she got to first, lunged at her, snarling like a vixen about to attack. 'And what the fuck you gonna to do about it, bitch?'

Vita head-butted her in the face, in the same way she'd always dreamed of doing to the evil little harlots during her own time at Cumnor Rise. The Girl fell back and landed motionlessly in the snow. Her two swooping henchwomen froze dead in their tracks. Vita looked up at them and glared, 'Get lost'. They obeyed and made off down the hill, leaving their ringleader alone and abandoned. Vita looked down at her third victim. Her eyes were ajar, blood trickled from her broken nose. 'Some friends you have,' Vita sniggered.

She returned to Joshua. He was okay, they hadn't hurt him. They'd just taken off one of his arms and stuck it in an obscene place. Vita quickly amended the damage and resumed: first she gave him a nose, a carrot from the refrigerator, then some eyes - or rather some sunglasses, so he wasn't blinded by the sun; carefully she dressed him in Arnold's brown suede jacket, his matching cap and then wrapped the auburn scarf around his neck. She stood back and looked at him, smiling.

He looked divine.

And then, it happened.

It really happened.

Tchaikovsky's *Waltz of the Flowers* really did start playing, drowning out the whole of West Oxfordshire. Vita's dark cloak magically turned into a long, beautiful ball gown, her winter boots into Cinderella's slippers. Then finally, Joshua came to life. Two little legs sprouted from beneath him and he hobbled away from where he stood. He looked at Vita, smiled and offered her one of his hands. She accepted. And, twirling her across their snowy dance floor, he spun her around and around. Then he swanned her across the hill as the music continued to play, over and over again.

It was just like that film, *The Snowman*, but even better. That was pretend. A children's story. This was real. Real! A real story of true love!

Vita had never been so happy.

She'd finally found the one.

Then Joshua stopped. Vita looked at him. Still holding her by the hand, he gently ascended into the sky, taking his new found love with him. She looked down as the Hurst grew smaller and smaller. Joshua stretched out his wooden arm and led her through the sky, over Osney Island, over Divinity College, over the river Cherwell and then, up into the clouds… leading to a world - far away from Oxford's spires - where everything was made of ice and the snow never stopped falling.

Joshua and Vita carefully touched down on an iceberg floating in a large pond, not dissimilar to the pond in University Parks. Swans floated across the icy water. Polar bears played amongst the wintry woodlands. There was not a human in sight. The music returned. Joshua resumed swaying Vita across the island. They danced for hours and hours and hours… she smiled, she laughed, she held him as tightly as she could, while he continued spinning her around and around…

But then the music stopped.

She was back on the Hurst.

The snow was no longer falling.

Her ball-gown had morphed back into her dark cloak.

Her Cinderella slippers had crumpled back into her walking boots.

Vita looked up at the evening sun slicing its scorching way through the icy air. Her eyes moved back to Joshua. He'd now returned to the place where she'd built him, and was looking sad, slumping forward and beginning to trickle away. She ran towards him and embraced him tightly.

'No, no, please don't go,' she begged, as he fell apart in her hands. And she pleaded with Mother Nature to take her as well. But it wasn't long before Joshua had succumbed to the milder temperature and was reduced to nothing but a pile of slushy wet clothes. Vita lay amongst his remains for some time, covered in mud, shivering from the cold, lost in her own despair.

A blackbird sang. The trees rustled. A crow squawked. The shrubs whispered.

But then her pain was interrupted by a terrible sound. Sitting up, Vita turned and looked in its direction as it screamed slowly but surely towards her from beyond the hills.

… A police siren.

ALONG FOR THE RIDE

MARGARET PELLING

'Keep going along the track from Moreton to Tetsworth and you will be sure to find the Swan,' his friends had said. That must be the Swan Hotel ahead of him, that great looming building, its lights shining out like beacons in the darkness. Dare he go inside and warm himself? No, no, he was still too close to Thame, the militia must be looking for him by now, they'd doubtless already been here and put people on their guard. An inn like this on the turnpike road to London was one of the first places they would come. Nothing for it but to forget how cold and wet he was and slip aboard one of the coaches in the yard.

There was one such near the road with the horses already in harness and passengers climbing in. But was it London-bound? He couldn't ask, he would have to risk it. Picking his moment, he tucked his bag under one arm, sprang lightly up onto the boot and from there to the roof, and crouched down behind the luggage in case the coachman or the man beside him on the box turned their heads and saw him. Thank God there were no passengers up here. Immediately, a deep voice powerful enough to carry over the wind and rain shouted, 'Away we go, beauties!' and the vehicle lurched out of the yard.

On top of a coach, the one thing necessary was to hang on for all one was worth to avoid being jolted off. There was one profession upon earth that taught a man how to survive at precarious heights while frozen and drenched to the skin: *la Marine*. Heaven be praised for *la Marine*.

The coach did not turn toward London, where he could have concealed himself in the crowds until he found a boat. He was being taken farther west. *Bougre!* From what he had learned of this locality, the next stop would be Oxford.

Nearly there. Joshua King raised his whip in salute to the tollgate keeper as the man opened the St Clements gate to let the coach through. Only the bridge to cross now, and then they'd be in the High Street and journey's end, at least for this day, would be all but reached.

'Here we are then, Billy,' shouted Joshua to his guard Billy Williams as the Angel Inn came into view, trying to make himself heard above the roaring wind and drenching rain. Collar up high and hat jammed down on his head so that he could scarcely see, he turned the coach into the courtyard of the Angel more by luck than judgement. By God, it was a filthy night. He was getting too old for the coaching business. Still, he had a few hours' respite before he had to start for Gloucester. Nancy would have a welcome for him: a nice fire, a mug of ale, a hot pie and later on, if he was lucky…

He clambered down from the box, every joint aching fit to break. In the old days he would have jumped. 'King of the Road,' that was him back then. Ah, those were the days.

He opened the door of the coach and pulled down the steps. 'Oxford, ladies and gentlemen,' he shouted. There were groans and yawns from inside. Nobody was making much attempt to step out. Well, he'd give them a minute or two to wake up, lucky buggers frowsting in there while he'd been trying to keep this vehicle out of the ditches for mile after mile. He wasn't going to stand here though. He'd go inside and warm himself while the ostlers unharnessed the horses. 'Come on, Billy,' he shouted. They'd come back out later and see to the luggage of the ones who were stopping here.

'Oh, Mr King, we'd almost given you up,' cried Nancy.

'You know me, Mrs Rawlinson, when have I ever been beaten by the weather?' She always called him Mr King in front of customers, and nothing other than 'Mrs Rawlinson' would do from him for this respectable widow who was housekeeper of the grandest establishment in Oxford.

'Come over here by the fire and warm yourself,' she said.

'I know something better than a fire I'd like to warm myself on,' he dared to murmur in her ear.

'Oh, get away with you,' she said in a low voice, but it had a laugh full of promise in it. 'Now, how many have you got for us tonight?' she went on as his cargo of wayfarers began to troop into the parlour.

'Half a dozen,' he said. 'Governesses and lawyers' clerks by the look of 'em. They won't need your best rooms, by any means.'

'Nasty night, ladies and gentlemen,' said Nancy as his passengers made their way towards the fire. Then a frown appeared on her forehead, which was odd, because she was the one person he knew who never frowned. 'Half a dozen, you say? There're seven newcomers in this room, not six.'

Eh? He counted them. She was right. There were seven bodies huddling round the fire, not counting Billy. At one side of the group, a little way from the others, was a figure muffled in a greatcoat with its face scarcely visible. It had the height and breadth of a man. 'Well, well,' he muttered. 'What have we here?' Tucked into his belt was the pistol he never went anywhere without. He patted it as he walked toward the stranger.

He joined the group by the fire, positioning himself by the stranger's shoulder. 'Just come in on the coach from London, have you, sir?' he said in a low voice.

'Indeed I have. What a very cold night,' said the man, not turning to him. He seemed to be having difficulty getting the words out. That wasn't hard to credit, seeing as how his teeth were chattering fit to break.

'Well, ain't that a thing,' said Joshua quietly, leaning towards the man. 'I'm the driver, you see. My eyes ain't quite as good as they were when I was younger, but I didn't see you get on, good sir.'

'I did not make a great display of myself,' said the man, almost too low for Joshua to hear. He had the sound of a gentleman but there was a faint twang in his speech. Like he hadn't grown up hearing the English language overmuch. He had a bag clutched in his arms as if it had the Crown Jewels in it.

By God.

'I'm not surprised,' said Joshua. 'For I think I know what you are.'

'Please,' said the man, and he turned his face to Joshua at last. There was such a look in his eyes: fear, pleading, desperation, defiance. Above all, defiance. And such eyes: large, dark, like deep pools in his pale face that was shrivelled with the cold. His hair was dark too, a mass of black curls. He was young, not above five and twenty by the look of him.

Nancy was beginning to take the other passengers into the dining room for a late supper. She gave Joshua a look. He shook his head. 'I'll stay a while longer with this gentleman till we've both thawed out,' he said.

When the parlour was clear, Joshua looked at the young man, he looked at him hard. 'Well now, I am Joshua King, and I've just told you I'm a coach driver. Now tell me exactly who you are and where you think you're going. And before you start, you can hand over any weapons you might have about you.' He let the young man have a sight of his pistol.

The man looked away and stretched out his hands to the fire. 'I am not armed,' he said, sounding weary. Then he straightened his back. 'Ensign Joseph de Bonnefoux of the *Marine Imperiale*, at your service.' He bowed at Joshua, then smiled. 'Or if you prefer, Prisoner Bonnefoux of the Thame Parole Depot. And where do I think I'm going?' He shrugged. 'Away from Thame. Back to France. It comes to the same thing.'

'Taken at Trafalgar, were you?'

The man shivered. 'No, thank God, not in that sea of blood.'

'Well, you won't get to France in a hurry coming by Oxford, young sir.'

'Beggars cannot be choosers, is not that what you English say? Yours was the first coach to leave the Swan at Tetsworth. I jumped aboard, climbed onto the top, and *voilà*, here I am.'

'You thought you'd come along for the ride, did you? Lucky for you my guard was riding up front with me, not at the back where he should have been.'

'That man was your guard?'

'Aye. Billy's taken to riding alongside me if there's nobody up top and nothing in the strongbox. He likes the company. Poor old Billy. He's like me, he's not really up to this work any more - he feels the cold too much. Any colder tonight, and we might've had to chip you off the roof.'

The young man smiled. 'I was once mast-headed all-night in weather worse than this.'

'You'll get put in the hulks if they catch you.'

The man's smile faded. '*Monsieur*, I was already destined for the hulks. That is why I ran away: I have nothing to lose. Are you going to call a constable? Are you going to let them catch me?'

'That depends. Why don't you and I sit down, and when Nancy comes back I'll get her to bring us some ale and pies, and maybe a couple of pipes, and you can tell me all about it.'

Bonnefoux reached inside his coat and pulled out the packet. He took out the lock of hair and held it up to the firelight. It glowed like spun gold. Taking a sip of ale, he said, 'It is not all bad in Thame for a prisoner on parole. There are kind people, such as the Luptons and the Stratfords.'

'Who did that belong to - Miss Lupton?' said the big coachman, indicating the lock of hair.

'Miss Jane Lupton is very agreeable, but no, this is from

Miss Harriet Stratford, of the blue eyes, the fair complexion, the lively voice, the… everything. I think it is as well that I had to run away, otherwise I would have asked her to marry me, and I am too young to marry. I have done very little in life yet… But I shall not forget her.' He kissed the lock of hair and put it back inside his coat. 'And I shall not forget Miss Lupton. She wrote such a pretty verse about my sparrow.' He sighed. 'I hope she will take care of it. I am sad to think of it coming to visit, and not finding me…'

'Did these ladies teach you your English?'

Bonnefoux grinned. 'I speak it well, do I not? Yes, the ladies helped, but I have been learning all the time in the months since I was captured. I had some English already - many of us do - but there is nothing like having to spend all your waking hours with those who speak it as natives. I am an excellent mimic, they tell me. With a little more practice I might even pass for an Englishman.'

As he would have to if he were to stay free.

'All very fine, I'm sure, but there must have been a mishap,' said the coachman.

'There were two mishaps. I said that Thame is not all bad, but there is a class there that does not like Frenchmen. The workmen from the brickfields south of the town think they are patriots. I say they are ruffians, especially when drunk, and Thame has a great many alehouses for their convenience. I was walking quietly through the town with a friend when one of these individuals staggered out from the White Horse and hurled himself against me - on purpose, I tell you. He uttered some foul oaths, and naturally I pushed him as he had pushed me. Being too drunk to stand, he tumbled onto the ground with great cries, and his friends came running from inside the alehouse. Fortunately for my friend and myself, all the Frenchmen that were lodging in the Birdcage Inn nearby heard the noise and came out into the street, and - well. You may imagine the rest.'

'There was an almighty battle. Noses were twisted, heads were broken.'

'Indeed. I am pleased that in this instance, the French were victorious against the English. But I could not get justice. The Admiralty's Agent in Thame, Mr Smith, would not pursue the matter - for fear of what the workmen might do to him, I believe. From that occasion there was enmity between myself and Mr Smith.'

'And the second mishap?'

Bonnefoux sighed. 'I breached parole regulations. An English friend offered to take me on an outing to Windsor, and I allowed myself to be persuaded. A pleasant time was had - I even glimpsed your King - and we returned the next day. To my relief, my absence went unremarked. The visit was months ago, but this morning I was talking about it in the street, perhaps unwisely, with some friends. When I returned to my lodgings, the constable and two of his men were waiting for me.'

'Somebody heard you in the street and told the Agent?'

Bonnefoux smiled. 'I would dearly love to know who that was.'

'But you got away, or else you wouldn't be here.'

'I asked to collect my things. The constable gave permission, and I took the opportunity to leave my room by the window... There was a tree growing nearby. I threw down my bag, launched myself at a branch, climbed down, and ran. I hid with some compatriots until dusk, and then made my way to the Swan. You know the rest.'

'Do you have money?'

'Oh yes, money is not a difficulty, I have plenty. I should pay you for an outside seat from Tetsworth.'

The big man gave him a thoughtful look. 'I'll let you off this once,' he said.

'So that is my story,' said Bonnefoux. 'What are you going to do?' The coachman was kind hearted under that gruff exterior, unless his own exhausted senses were deceiving him.

The man yawned. 'What I'm going to do is sleep for a few hours,' he said. 'You should too. You can have my bed. There's another bed in the room, and my guard Billy Williams is in it, but don't you worry about him, he'll sleep the sleep of the dead until I come to wake him.'

'Thank you. But where will you sleep?'

'Never you mind about that,' said the man.

'Well, Josh, what are you going to do about him?' said Nancy.

'You're thinking I should do my duty as an Englishman and turn him over to the authorities,' said Joshua, rolling onto his back.

She sighed. 'But then he'll go to those filthy prison hulks and rot - and die, as like as not. Poor young man.'

He took a long breath. She'd put her finger on it. Poor young man, indeed. 'Maybe in the morning we'll find him gone,' he said.

For a moment or so she didn't say anything. 'Just as well a place like this hardly has time to close its doors at night,' she said at last.

She was right there. Trade came and went at all hours. If anybody could find an unlocked door or even window and make himself scarce, he'd wager that young man he'd been talking to certainly could.

Soon, the regular breathing from the other side of the bed told him that she was asleep. By rights he ought to be asleep too, but he had the feeling that sleep was going to be hard to come by this night.

If he did his duty, a pleasant young man was in for some right harsh treatment. But if Englishmen let French prisoners walk free because they were pleasant, they'd be back in their own country and fighting Englishmen again before you could say Jack Robinson. The English sailors who'd died in action against that young man's ship would have lost their lives in vain. The trouble was, though, once you'd met one of them and seen he was just a man like you…

What would Mr Burton do? Joshua's mind began to reach back into the past…

A Norfolk vicar, leading the quietest life imaginable, finds in his orchard one moonlit night a desperate young man, not much more than a boy. There's a hue and cry in the distance, and it's coming this way. 'Put that pistol away and come inside,' says Mr Burton. He shelters the young man until all is quiet, telling the constable: 'No, no one has passed this way at all.' And then he and the young man spend the rest of the night in hard talk…

And because of Mr Burton, Joshua King is here now, next to a sleeping woman who's still lovely despite her years, not lying where they bury gallows-fodder. Joshua King mended his ways and left the bad company he'd been keeping and became Mr Burton's under-groom. He mended his manners and his speech along with his ways, and he found he had such a knack with horses and carriages that he got himself a post as a stagecoach driver. After a while, he started to drive the mails. Those were the glory days! All the girls around Lombard Street would flock in the evenings to watch the mail coaches setting off from the Post Office, and no driver got more admiring stares than the King of the Road.

'You were a good man, Mr Burton,' he said softly, 'you were the best man I ever knew, God rest your soul. If you can speak from beyond the grave, tell me what to do.'

But there was no word from Mr Burton. The first voices he heard were from the birds as the dawn came up.

Joshua dressed quickly. He had to be out of Nancy's room before the manager came looking for her, and he had to be on the box of his coach in fifteen minutes. As he dressed, he chewed mouthfuls of the bread Nancy had brought him and washed it down with draughts of coffee. He'd take some of this along to Billy in a minute. Nancy put her head out of the room and looked up and down the corridor. 'Nobody's about,' she whispered.

Joshua slipped out and along to his room. Please God let the young man be gone.

Ensign Bonnefoux wasn't gone. He was sitting on his bed looking at Billy Williams. Billy was still asleep as usual, but he was tossing and turning and moaning.

'I fear he is not well, your colleague,' said Bonnefoux quietly. 'He has been like that for hours. I think a physician should be sent for.'

'He's taken a chill, what with that rain yesterday. Well, it looks as if I'll be riding without a guard today. I'll go and tell Nancy.' But as he stepped into the corridor, there was Nancy coming running.

'We've got the militia downstairs,' she gasped. 'They're searching everywhere in Oxford for him.' She jerked her head in the direction of Bonnefoux.

'*O Dieu*,' whispered Bonnefoux, hanging his head.

It was the look on his face. Never had Joshua seen a man look so much the way he himself had felt back in Mr Burton's orchard all those years ago. 'Here,' he said, throwing him Billy's greatcoat. 'Put this on. Put your own coat on first, mind - you're of a height with Billy but he's broader than you.'

Bonnefoux didn't take long to catch on. Billy's heavy coach guard's coat was on him in a trice. His own hat would do, it was nondescript enough.

'Now take this,' said Joshua, handing him Billy's blunderbuss. 'Nancy'll show you down the back stairs and into the yard. There's my coach, they're just putting the horses to it.' He pointed through the window. 'Just saunter out there, as easy as you please, and climb up onto the box - like a man past fifty would, mind, not a spry young fellow like you. Keep your hat down. With luck, nobody'll take any notice of you. Don't say anything, they won't be expecting it. Billy's dumb, you see.'

'Thank you, thank you,' gasped Bonnefoux.

'You can thank me when we're well out of Oxford. Now get out to that coach.'

They were passing Eynsham before Joshua dared to take a breath.

'May I thank you now?' said the young man beside him on the box.

'You may,' said Joshua. 'Now, when we get to Gloucester, your best bet is to hire a chaise and make your way to London but by a roundabout route. Go through Chippenham, Basingstoke and Guildford, say.'

There was a minute's silence, and then: 'Why are you doing this for me?'

Joshua thought for a moment. 'Because I was young once, that's why.'

Historical Notes

Ensign Pierre Marie Joseph de Bonnefoux-Beauregard of the frigate Belle Poule was taken prisoner after an action on 13 March 1806 between a British squadron commanded by Admiral Sir John Borlase Warren and a much smaller French force commanded by Admiral Charles Linos, consisting only of Linois' flagship Marengo and the Belle Poule.

Officer prisoners were allowed to live as ordinary citizens on parole in British country towns, subject to certain restrictions on their movements. Bonnefoux was allocated to Thame. After many adventures, the intelligent and enterprising Bonnefoux made his way back to France, where he resumed his naval career. He became Baron de Bonnefoux in 1847. For this story, I have drawn on his published Memoires.

The Victoria Fountain on the Plain in East Oxford stands on the site of the former St Clements toll house. Most of the Angel Inn was demolished in 1876 to make way for the University of Oxford's Examination Schools. Two bays remain in the High Street, however, one housing the Grand Café. The Swan at Tetsworth now functions as an antiques centre as well as a pub. The White Horse in Thame is now a hardware shop, but the Birdcage Inn is still one of the most prominent pubs in the town.

HOME FOR CHRISTMAS

JANE STEMP

... It's a long way to Tipperary, It's a long way to go ...

He whistled as he walked away from Oxford Station, pack slung over one shoulder not at all according to regulations. Homecoming made the way seem shorter, although the road from the station was as long as ever, the reflections in the canal where Hythe Bridge Street crossed it as cold and deep as ever. The ironworks, still named for William Lucy although the old man had died more than forty years ago, clanked and burned like a corner of hell in Walton Well Road. No ironwork any more; they made munitions now. He hurried past.

His mother's welcome was warm, although the house was cold; even the house was warmer than Flanders. And drier; but anything would be drier than the bitter mud of Passchendaele.

'Tom!' Her face was lit with joy. 'Oh my boy, my lad, I never thought - why didn't you write and tell me?'

'I did write, Mum,' he said. 'The letter'll turn up some day. In time for next Christmas, most like.' He grinned. 'Oh, *Mum*, it's good to see you.' He flung his arms round her as if he was nine again and not nineteen, and held her tight, duster and all, until she batted him off with her free hand.

'Tom, give over, you'll have my feet off the floor - mind you, I feel like I'm walking on air already. I'd have cleaned the house better if I'd known.'

'And me treading the mud in over your white doorstep just the same,' Tom said, smiling. He had grown, since last time when he came on leave. Now he could see the top of her head, even when she was standing up.

'For once in a while, never mind the doorstep. Come in,

sit down. I'll put the kettle on.' She moved across the hall, uncertainly, from one doorway to another.

'Mum,' he said, '*Not* the parlour. Kitchen'll do me. Come on.'

After the cold brown paint of the hallway, the kitchen, with its pale scrubbed table and the white enamel shining, was almost warm. Tom said, 'How is everyone, Mum?'

'Not too bad, considering.' She hesitated. 'You heard about Fred Meakin?'

'I heard.'

'And, Mrs Barron over the road, her Eric came back with what she won't say, and he's still in hospital down South. She doesn't hardly get to see him since they sent the money for her first visit.' The kettle began to hiss on the range.

'That's bad,' he said. 'I like Eric.'

Her joy was still shining off her. 'But *you're* home, Tom, you're home. Oh, we'll have such a Christmas, you and me and your father.'

He laughed. 'What - turkey and chestnuts and brandy, like we were generals in the mess?'

'What would we be doing with turkey? There'll be a ham from Hedges same as usual. But I got my pudding made and waiting.'

He looked round the kitchen. 'You haven't decorated yet.'

'The holly's in the back yard. I'm not bringing it and bad luck into the house together.' His mother handed him a mug of tea. 'You know it's not Christmas Eve until tomorrow. There, get that down you, love.'

'Isn't it? I lose track of the days.' He wrapped his fingers round the mug, and blew. The steam drifted into the air and faded like smoke. Like - no, he would not think about it.

She turned her back and said, 'Is it bad, Tom? Out there?'

The fire crackled in the range. He was glad she wasn't looking at him. At last he peeled his lips open and said, 'I get by. You don't want to know, Mum.'

'Your father will, when he comes off the back-shift at Lucy's.'

'Maybe.' He put one hand on her shoulder and turned her to face him. 'Look, Mum, I'm smiling, see? I'll do.'

'I believe you.' She reached up and patted his cheek. 'Your father'll be so glad.'

He drained his mug, and said, 'Maybe I should call on Mrs Barron?'

'She'll take it kindly, I'm sure. And - ' his mother looked at him under her lashes - 'Elsie Meakin is home for Christmas. Poor lass, she was that cut up when the news about Fred came in, he being her oldest brother, and they having no father any more.'

Tom nodded. 'I wrote to her. Mrs Meakin wrote back to say thank you. I'm glad Elsie's home, though.' His hand strayed to one pocket. 'I bought her - oh, never mind. Anything I can help you with?'

'Nothing. You go right along to Hart Street, my boy, and stay as long as you like.'

The front door banged again ten minutes later, and quick footsteps sounded through the house. When Tom's mother came into the kitchen again, on the table was a small package, the brown paper crumpled and coming adrift, showing a corner of white lace and an embroidered E. The back door was open.

'Tom? Didn't you see Elsie?'

He was in the back yard, up to his ankles in holly thorns, the tower of St Barnabas pointing to the sky behind his shoulder. 'I saw her. She wouldn't let me in. Wouldn't talk to me. Because I came back, and not Fred.'

'Oh, Tom. Oh, that's - '

'It's not anything,' he said. 'I understand.' He stood there, a branch of holly in his hands, staring at it. 'I did more than hear about Fred. I was there, you see. He was blown to pieces.

And there was blood.' He picked the berries one by one from the branch, and hurled them one by one across the yard. 'In drops. Like rain. Like this.'

The branch was bare of everything but the twisted, thorny leaves; he let it fall. As his mother took his shaking hands, a single berry rolled inside the door.

A CUP OF COFFEE

GINA CLAYE

Anna was determined to relax. She sank back on the chair, took a deep breath and let it out slowly.
'Sit comfortably.'
The voice on the tape was quiet but distinct.
'Let your body feel heavy.'
She didn't feel heavy, she felt wound up.
'Let all the tension go, in each part of your body.'
Why was it so difficult to relax? She uncrossed her legs and let her hands drop in her lap.
'Let your thoughts, your current preoccupations disappear. Pay attention to your breathing. Be still.'
She *was* paying attention to her breathing but it wasn't working. Why couldn't she relax? She'd had a cup of camomile tea before coming out instead of the usual coffee. Okay, she'd had a rush to get here but thank goodness she'd managed to park just outside the Friends Meeting House. Empty parking places in St Giles were usually non existent.

She pulled herself up. She was thinking and she shouldn't be. She was supposed to let her thoughts disappear... At least the chairs were comfortable here in the garden room. She loved the benches in the old Quaker Meeting house but these chairs were better for relaxing in or rather trying to. It was breezy outside, stirring the leaves of the ancient tree she loved sitting under. She could see the Meeting House at the bottom of the garden. She closed her eyes tightly. She shouldn't be looking out.
'Wait.'
The voice of the prompt made her jump.
'In this receptive state of mind, let the real concerns of your life emerge. Pay attention to what is going on inside you. Wait.'

Right, she must clear her mind so she could find out what was going on inside her. She took another deep breath and tried not to think of anything. Was anybody else finding this as hard as she was? She risked a peep at the others. They all looked very relaxed and distant, one had taken her shoes off. All had their eyes closed. They'd been coming to Experiment with Light for a good while; this was the first time she'd tried it. Apparently it was 'a process of self discovery, helping us to see ourselves in a new way and with this insight to know what steps to take in order to act effectively and find peace of mind'. At least that's what she'd read. She'd thought it might be a bit like the Mindfulness people went on about.

She was ready for the next prompt.

'Pay attention. Let what is inside you, in other words, the Light, show you what is important, or tough just now. Focus on one issue. Try to get a sense of this thing as a whole. Deep down you know what it is about but you don't normally allow yourself to take it all in and absorb the reality of it. Now is the time to do so.'

Thoughts still chased across her mind but she also began to feel a slight sense of unease. Nothing she could put into words. But it was definitely there.

'Let the answer come. And when it does, let a word or image also come that says what it's really like, this thing that concerns you.'

She lent back in her chair, her breathing calmer now... 'A word or image'... The feeling of unease increased...

She let her breath out slowly; there was a smell, a smell of coffee.

'Now ask yourself what makes it like that. Don't try to explain it. Just wait in the Light till you can see what it is. Let the full truth reveal itself, or as much truth as you are able to take at this moment.'

A half empty cup of coffee lay on the table before her. Where was she?

'When the answer comes, welcome it. It may be painful or difficult to believe with your normal conscious mind, but if it is the truth you will recognise it immediately. You will realise that it's something you need to know. Trust the Light. Say yes to it. It will show you new possibilities. It will show you the way through. So however the news seems to be at first, accept it and let its truth pervade your whole being.'

A face, one she recognised, a face that disturbed her...

'As soon as you accept what is being revealed to you, you will begin to feel different. Accepting truth about yourself is like making peace. Something is being resolved. If none of this seems to have happened, do not worry. It may take longer.'

A memory. They'd been sitting in Blackwell's cafe together. She couldn't remember what she'd said but she'd abandoned the rest of her coffee, hurried down the stairs and threaded her way through the crowded bookshop. Then she was out, out in the fresh air...

The words came as a shock to her.

'When you feel ready, open your eyes, stretch your limbs, and bring the meditation to an end.'

Anna closed the door and stepped out into the sunshine, a welcome change after all the rain they'd had. She may have left the Meeting house behind but the intense unease that the Experiment with Light had aroused was still with her. Even after the quarter of an hour silence at the end when she'd gone into the kitchen to get herself a glass of water, taking care not to talk to anyone, as she'd been told, she still felt unsettled as though something was churning inside her. Although some of the others had shared their experience with the rest of the group, she hadn't wanted to, which she was assured was fine.

She crossed over to her car and threw her anorak on the back seat, then took her water bottle out of her bag and had a few mouthfuls. She could still see that face... She pulled herself together and had another swig of water. That was better, now for the Ashmolean. She might as well pop into the Egyptian section of the museum and look at the exhibits there so she could prepare for the visit of her year 4 class next Thursday. She started to walk down St Giles, past the Eagle and Child. She shivered, despite the sunshine; the memory had really unsettled her - that smell of coffee…

She caught sight of an ice cream sign outside one of the shops. Better not, she thought, they wouldn't let me into the Ashmolean licking a cornet. As she walked on her mind drifted back. She hadn't expected the Experiment with Light to be anything but a meditative sit down. She pulled herself together, she didn't want to think about it.

She turned and walked up the steps to the Ashmolean. At least she could kill two birds with one stone today; she wouldn't have to make another journey into Oxford. Pushing open the door she made her way down the Randolph gallery. That face, that conversation. The painful episode was quite a while ago, some time last year, and although they'd waved from across the road they hadn't spoken since.

She turned into the entrance to the Egyptian section. It was a relief to be doing a task for school. She could forget the whole Experiment with Light episode.

She moved over to the glass cases on her left, searching for artefacts that her pupils might find interesting. They were objects found in graves in Predynastic Egypt, the very early period. Her attention was caught by a red pottery beaker decorated with white triangles and animals. The animals were very simple. One of the larger ones had horns and a mane hanging down from its chest. She remembered drawing animals similar to these when she was a child - she hadn't made much progress since.

'Excuse me, could you move your rucksack to the front. If you have it on your back you might knock into things.' The woman, obviously an official, looked apologetic. Anna swung her rucksack to the front obediently and wandered through to the next room. On her left were objects from The Old Kingdom, about 2570 BC. One that stood out was a coffin board carved with hieroglyphs which had once been painted white although only a few traces of paint were left. She stared at it. Someone now dead had done this fantastic work thousands of years ago and it had survived.

Slowly she turned away. On the wall to the right was a line. She made her eyes focus on it and attempted to take in the words. It was a time line dating from the Predynastic period to Roman times with pictures of objects dating from the particular period underneath, all very clearly explained. This would be perfect for her class.

She didn't look too closely at the large shrine of King Taharqa. It was very dark inside; the children could investigate it. She rounded the corner of the shrine and saw the case with the mummy ahead. Several children in school uniform were holding white boards up against the glass and were drawing on small pieces of paper. On closer observation she saw that they were pieces of papyrus. She must get some of those for her class. She stood undecided. She couldn't get near the case while the children were there. She looked around. There was a kind of window grille thing down to the right, and more pots further along. She couldn't make up her mind.

The teacher was beckoning the children on. Slowly, comparing drawings they moved away. Anna made her way to the case. It was the coffin of Djeddjehutyiuefankh, she read, a Theban priest. What a name! She made herself look closely at the contents. She needed to tell the children what to look out for. There were painted wooden figures of falcons representing the sky god, Horus; they'd been studying him, and a painted statuette of a jackal representing the god, Wepwawet, who guarded the dead. She shivered but forced herself to make a few notes, then turned away in relief.

She found herself looking at a case full of jewellery. Obviously a body like the one lying behind her had once decorated their then living body with these necklaces, these bracelets… The blue necklace was uncannily like one she had at home, one she'd inherited a long time ago.

The next case contained scrolls of papyrus. They were about inheritance. She began to read the papyrus nearest her. It described two acts of adoption by a childless couple.

She needed to go to the loo. She must find the Ladies. She'd passed a sign on the way in to the Egyptian section. She hurried back the way she'd come. She stumbled down the first few steps before catching hold of the handrail. Yes, there it was, thank goodness.

As Anna came out she saw the doors to the cafe on the other side of the steps. The smell of coffee was almost overpowering. It drew her towards it. Thankfully there were only a couple of people queuing. She made her way to a small table and sank into the chair. She took a sip of the hot coffee and felt the warmth travel down her body. Her tense muscles began to relax. She hunted for a tissue and blew her nose, she wasn't going to cry, she wasn't. But she couldn't help it, the tears rolled down her cheeks. Blindly she felt for her cup and held it. She inhaled the smell of the coffee, she didn't want to go on remembering, but she couldn't help it.

They'd met downstairs in Blackwell's. She'd come to get Patrick Gale's new book and had come across Jen waiting at the till. They lived in the same village. She didn't know her very well but they went to the same church and Anna knew that she'd recently been bereaved. Chatting, they'd both decided they needed a cup of coffee so made their way upstairs to the cafe…

'There's nothing like a cup of coffee after a couple of hours shopping.'

'Absolutely,' agreed Anna and took another mouthful of the *hot restoring liquid. 'Are you going on Saturday?'*

'Saturday?'

'You know, the protest against the closure of the library.'

'Oh that... I may do,' said Jen. 'It depends how I'm feeling.'

'I'm definitely going,' said Anna.

In the lull that followed, Jen delved in her bag and brought out a book. 'I wanted to get this because it's got a poem which a friend read at the remembrance service for my mother,' she said.

'Yes, I'm so sorry to hear about your loss,' Anna responded.

Jen sat silently reading it and tears began to fall down her cheeks. She did nothing to check them, but went on reading.

Anna began to feel uncomfortable. Should she say something?

Jen closed the book and took a tissue out from her pocket. 'Sorry,' she said, 'it just takes me like this sometimes. It was such a shock. Nobody knew she had anything wrong with her heart. It just happened without warning. I found her. I dropped in to see if she needed anything from the shop and I found her lying on the kitchen floor. I just can't believe it... We were so close. I can't believe it's happened.'

Anna searched frantically for words. 'I can understand how you must feel,' she said at last.

Jen stopped wiping her eyes and looked at her with an expression on her face that Anna couldn't fathom.

'You'll get over it,' she added. She really couldn't cope with this.

'How can you possibly understand,' Jen blurted out. 'Your mother hasn't died.'

'You're upset. I'll get you another coffee,' was all Anna could find to say. She had to get away.

Luckily it didn't take long. She paid for the coffee and hurried with it back to the table. 'I'm sorry,' she muttered as she put the cup down, 'I must go. I've got an appointment. I do hope you'll be alright.' But she couldn't look Jen in the face and hurried off without another word, down the stairs, through the *crowded bookshop, and out into the fresh air...*

Someone was wiping the table. 'Sorry to disturb you,' said the woman, 'there's some coffee spilt.'

Anna watched the blue and white cloth soak it up, her mind brought back to the present. It had been the Experiment with Light that had uprooted the memories. But it was the contents of the papyrus in the last Egyptian case that had finally jolted her back into the past...

Adoption.

She had been adopted. It had happened when she was still quite young. There had been a car crash. Both her mother and father had been killed and she'd been adopted by her childless aunt and uncle. She remembered the unwillingness of her aunt and uncle to discuss it. 'We must move on,' they had insisted. So she'd moved on, she'd got over it. And buried her grief.

Her tears spilled down her cheeks. Jen wasn't the only one. *She* had lost her mother and her father too. She let the tears come, not caring who saw. It was a relief, finally, to admit it to herself. To be able at last to start grieving.

'Accepting truth about yourself is like making peace.' The words from Experiment with Light echoed through her mind. She wouldn't try and avoid Jen any more. In fact she would take the very next opportunity to speak to her. She would apologise for so suddenly abandoning her in Blackwell's. If she explained, Jen would understand, as she finally did herself. She would invite her over one morning and they could have a good chat, a heart to heart... a cup of coffee.

Historical Notes

In 1994 Rex Ambler, a Quaker, was pondering on the spiritual experience that gave 17th Century Quakers such joy and peace of mind and the courage to share it with others even when beaten and imprisoned for doing so. He began to suspect that, hidden in their words, was a particular spiritual practice.

While Rex was exploring the experiences of early Quakers, he was introduced to the work of the American psychologist Eugene Gendling which is called 'Focusing'. The Quaker Experiment with Light meditation uses a set of very similar steps to this. It is a modern interpretation of the meditative spiritual practice of early Quakers.

THE WITCHING STONES

LIZ HARRIS

Old St Bartholomew's Day, 10th October, 1850s

The two girls pulled their crocheted shawls more tightly around their shoulders and hurried along the dried-mud track in the direction of Chipping Norton, carefully avoiding the deep ruts made by the hooves of cows. High above them, the early morning song of the robin mingled with the cackling of hens that rose from the distant outhouses.

The air was yet raw, and a thin layer of milk-white frost sheened the blue-black elderberries and ripe purple blackberries that hung from the thorny brambles, blackthorn and wild privet that flanked the wayside.

'We're nearly at the crossroads now,' Annie said as the hedgerows gave way to a line of workers' cottages, their weathered stone walls gleaming in the burgeoning light of the sun. Glints of gold danced off the gabled windows set into the tiled roofs.

Margaret stared anxiously ahead. 'William will be wonderin' where we are. He might even have given up and gone. 'Tis a cold morning to be standin' long at the crossroads.'

'As sure as the Mop Fair is on today, he won't have done,' Annie said firmly. 'He knows we had to light the fires, shake out the carpet, polish the dining-room furniture, and clean the boots and front steps before we left the big house. He'll wait for us. And anyway, the sun's now startin' to warm the air.'

Margaret glanced quickly at her friend. 'You sound very sure of him. I'm wonderin' if you've got an understandin' with him you haven't told me about.'

Annie shook her head. 'I've only seen him on a few Sunday afternoons, haven't I, and nothin's yet been said by him. But he's goin' to ask me, I'm sure.'

'You're lucky. He's a quiet, sober man, and a skilled weaver. He'll not be wastin' his money on drink like my pa, and you'll always have food on your plate.'

'And a roof over my head as he's got a cottage of his own. It was passed down to him by his father, who was a god-fearin' man, William said. Apparently, the downstairs parlour's neatly furnished, with stairs leading up from it to a large room set in the roof. There's a window at each end and that's where his hand-looms are. Also there are two small bedrooms up there, each with whitewashed walls and a grate for a fire.' She beamed at Margaret. 'I never thought I'd have a sweetheart with a cottage. It makes me very content to walk out with William.'

'So you won't be going up to the Whispering Knights with us after the fair, then, will you? You don't need the stones to name your future husband.'

'Of course, I will,' Annie said lightly. 'Not to ask who I'll marry, but to know my fortune. And I might even chip off a bit of stone for good luck. You should do the same so that you, too, marry a good, hard-working man, and not a lazy ne'er-do-well. And there's nothing could make me miss the dancin' afterwards.'

Margaret nodded. 'Unless you've gone there to be hired, 'tis the best bit o' the Mop Fair. I'd never forgo it either.'

'Look, 'tis William!' Annie exclaimed a few minutes later. 'I said he'd wait.'

Their eyes on the man who stood at the crossroads staring towards them, a cloth cap on his head and a knee-length brown-wool coat over a grey buttoned waistcoat and dark blue trousers, they speeded up.

'You *are* lucky,' Margaret repeated, as they neared him.

By the time they reached Chipping Norton, the narrow streets lined with hawkers and pedlars were crowded with people heading for the market place, and the air was loud with the sound of music, laughter and shouting.

Annie felt her excitement grow.

'One moment,' Margaret said, and she bent down to tie the lace on her boot.

'May I say, the green of your dress becomes you, Annie?' William said quietly as they waited for Margaret. 'And the way you've done your hair.'

'Thank you,' Annie said, a blush rising to her cheeks. Looking quickly down, she smoothed her cotton calico dress and patted the hair she'd parted in the centre, her chestnut ringlets gathered on either side.

Margaret straightened up and they continued walking.

'I've been looking forward to today for a very long time,' Annie said, her eyes shining as she gazed around her.

William gave a slight cough. "Tis regrettable, but I'm unable to stay for long at the fair. I've cloth that must be finished this very day.'

'Oh, William!' Annie exclaimed, and she stopped walking and stared at him in dismay.

'I see I'll be goin' home alone, then,' Margaret said, throwing a sly glance at Annie. 'You won't want to stay after William's gone, will you, Annie? You've no need to ask the stones for the name of your sweetheart, and you won't want to stay for the dancin', will you?'

Blood rushed to Annie's cheeks.

'There're other reasons for goin' to the stones, like keepin' your friends company,' she said sharply. She heard a trace of defiance in her voice. 'But spending time with you, William, is more to my likin',' she added quickly, 'and I'll be leavin' when you do.'

'If you wish to stay longer, you must do so,' William said gravely. 'I've no wish to deny you the company of friends you're seldom able to see.'

"Tis generous of you to be so understanding, but of course I'll leave with you,' Annie muttered. Glancing to her right, she glared at Margaret, and they started to walk again.

Reaching the market place, they turned left, and stood in front of A.A.Webb & Sons, their backs to the iron-framed windows displaying haberdashery, china and toys. They stared at the throng of labourers hoping to be hired, a dark brown fustian haze flecked with the white of the smock-frocks worn by the shepherds.

All those seeking employment were either wearing or carrying something that showed their trade - carters and waggoners had a piece of whip-cord around their hats, shepherds carried a crook or some wool, cowmen some straw, dairymaids a milking stool or a pail, and housemaids a broom or a mop.

All the while, masters looking to hire workers threaded a path between the labourers, questioning them, and then handing over a shilling to seal the deal, whereupon the newly hired workers donned bright ribbons, whose patches of colour brought life to the market place.

As they watched the bargaining, the smell of stew cooking grew stronger. Drawn by the aroma, they turned away and headed for the hillside flanked with booths offering food, home-brewed beer, ale and cider. Reaching the stall where the stew was simmering in a metal cauldron that hung over a charcoal fire, they each asked for a ha'pennyworth, and stood there and ate it.

Their stew eaten, they strolled down side streets paved with cobblestones, lingering every so often to watch the strolling players, performing jugglers and the puppet shows.

At the first theatrical booth they came to, Annie laughingly urged William to peep inside it with her, but he refused. He didn't favour such forms of entertainment, he told her quietly. Annie hesitated a moment, but decided it would appear somewhat contrary to say you were going to do something, and then not do it, so she went in, but quickly come out again.

Margaret remained outside with William.

When they reached the big wooden wheel, which was turned by the hand of the man from a neighbouring village who'd made it, Annie refused to heed the reluctance on William's part, but insisted that he join her on it, so all three had a penny's worth turn of the wheel.

'I regret I must go now, Annie,' he said, stepping off the wheel and brushing himself down. 'But you may stay longer, if you wish. Though perhaps 'tis timely to leave the fair now. With the hired men's shillings being spent on drink, there'll soon be many a toper on the streets.'

Annie felt her spirits sink.

'Of course I'll come with you, William,' she said, trying to quash her disappointment. 'There are friends I would have wished to meet today, but I can see them next year.'

'Next year's fair will be a long time coming. You must stay to meet your friends,' William said. 'I'll not mind walking home alone.'

'Are you sure?' Annie tried to keep her enthusiasm from her voice.

He smiled at her. 'Don't give it head-room, Annie. I shall see you next Sunday afternoon. But for now, I bid you both good-day.' He doffed his cap to them, and made to move away.

'William!' Margaret suddenly called. 'I have a headache and would do well to leave now. Perhaps you would walk some of the way with me?'

'Indeed I will, Margaret,' he said. Again touching his cap to Annie, he turned away, and with Margaret at his side, went back down the hill.

Frowning, she stared at their retreating backs, wondering for a moment if she'd be wise to run after them and walk with

William, too.

'Annie!' she heard a voice call. Glancing across the street, she saw her friend, Mary.

Shrugging off her sudden formless concern, she ran over the road to join her.

Fortunately for the excited girls, there were sufficient lads with wagons who were willing to drive them up to the ridge as the afternoon drew to a close. Only as far as the ridge, the lads said firmly - they'd wait on the road with the wagons while the women went over the field to the stones.

Finding herself close to a blue wagon, Annie started walking towards it. Then she stopped sharply. She'd never before seen that lad in breeches, a waistcoat over his white shirt, a scrap of bright red cotton around his neck, who was leaning against the side of the blue wagon, his arms folded, his face tilted to the sun, and she wasn't sure whether she shouldn't wait for Mary to catch her up.

But the lad had seen her, and was straightening up and smiling in welcome, so she went forward and let him help her into the wagon.

He was a strong, handsome man, who looked as if he spent most of his time out of doors, she thought. As he indicated that she should stand next to the place where he'd be standing, she inhaled his scent of musky spice, leather and woodsmoke, and she felt herself colour slightly.

When the wagons were full, they set off in the slowly fading light of day, heading north through the town. As he drove, the waggoner told Annie his name was Jem. She asked how he came to be a waggoner. At the age of six, he started scaring crows for a farmer, he said, but it was a long, lonely day, and he didn't have any shelter, not even a small hut made of straw hurdles, so he was often drenched when he got home at night.

But things got better when he was twelve and was taken

on as a waggoner's mate. He boarded with the waggoner and his wife, and learned to turn his hand to anything on a farm.

'I've never shirked hard work,' he said, 'and I'm goin' to have a place of my own one day. First I'll rent a couple of furnished rooms, maybe in a row of cottages. But the day will come when I get my own small cottage.'

'My friend, William, has already got a cottage,' Annie told him proudly. 'He's a weaver. I expect to be promised to him soon.'

'I'd go mad bein' inside all day,' Jem said, urging the two horses forward along the winding path that sloped up the hill. The axles groaned and the wagon swayed, and Annie hung on tight. 'As for weaving,' he added, and he made a face of dislike. 'That clickety-clacking of machines from morning to night would send me crazy. I'd take the fields and open air any time, even if it meant having to scare the crows again.'

'Maybe so, but a weaver will always have work because people must wear clothes,' Annie retorted.

Jem shrugged. 'Everyone must eat, so I'll always have work, too, won't I?'

He turned and smiled at Annie, and she felt a strange sensation run down the length of her body.

Moments later, the wagons were as close to the stones as they could go, and the women started climbing down. Leaving the men at the road, they went past the stone circle of the king's men which stood on their right, and turned left along the path that ran between a wood and the open field, on the far side of which stood the Whispering Knights.

'It's really eerie here.' Mary's voice trembled as they drew near the four large stones that towered above a fifth that was lying on the ground between them, a thin grey mist swirling around the base of each.

Giggling nervously, they gathered in a group, standing far enough back so as not to hear what each girl said when she approached the stones.

'Looking at the stones, 'tis easy to believe they were once people,' Annie whispered.

'Ma doesn't believe that,' Mary said. 'She said 'tis a lie that a wicked witch called Mother Shipton tricked an ambitious king who wanted to be King of England, and then turned him and his soldiers to stone. I agree with Ma.'

'Well, I don't. And I also believe she saw five knights lagging behind, whispering to each other, plotting to overthrow the king, and turned them into stone, too, and then turned herself into an elder tree. Just look at the stones - they look like men!' she exclaimed, pointing at them.

When it was Annie's turn, she went up to the nearest stone, pressed her mouth hard against its cold surface to make sure it heard her correctly, and asked to be told her fortune. She heard a slight scuffling noise and then, as clearly as anything, she heard the stone say in a high-pitched sort of way that her life would be full of great happiness.

A rosy glow swept over her, chasing away the chill that had crept into the air. And then, to her great surprise, she asked something she hadn't intended to ask.

'Who will I marry?' she blurted out.

She drew back slightly and stared at the stone in bewilderment, not knowing why she'd asked that question - she knew she was going to marry William. She must have just been testing the stone to see how much it really knew, she decided, and she waited to hear William's name.

But the stone said Jem!

Jem was its answer.

How can that be, she thought. She was going to be a weaver's wife, and they were going to live in the weaver's cottage that his father had had before him. She must have misheard. After all, William sounded a bit like Jem if you only heard the end of it. So she leaned forward and said very politely that she didn't think she'd heard a-right, and would the stone please tell her again.

And it did.

And again it said Jem!

When she got back into the road, she couldn't look Jem in the eye. Instead, she went and stood at the back of the wagon. When they reached Chipping Norton, he helped them all from the wagon, she being the last to get down as she'd been at the back.

He looked at her, his face anxious, and said that the stones might have upset her as the smile had gone from her face and she looked worried. She swiftly assured him that they hadn't.

'Just to make sure,' he said, falling into step beside her, 'will you walk out with me on Sunday afternoon? Something is troubling you, and I feel responsible as I took you there. I'd like to help, if you'll let me.'

She opened her mouth to say she'd be walking with William, but then she remembered what the stones had said. Suddenly concerned that they might not like it if she didn't attempt to heed them, she found herself saying yes.

The amber flame from the tallow-candle in Annie's hand flickered, lifting the gloom of dusk from above the narrow bed and throwing restless shadows into the corners of the small bedroom. Moving closer to the bed, she gazed down at the three small children lying close to each other beneath their loosely woven wool blanket, their sleeping faces glistening.

There was a sound from the other side of the partition wall, and the door between the two bedrooms opened. Annie glanced across at her husband of almost ten years and smiled at him.

'What did the children ask to hear this evening?' he asked, coming into the room.

'The story of the Mop Fair.'

'Again?' he exclaimed in mock horror.

'Yes, again,' she said, laughing as she looked up at him, her face shining in the candlelight.

'Don't they ever tire of that story?'

'No, never; and I never tire of telling it. Every time I talk about that day, I go back there in my head. The stones didn't lie when they promised me happiness, and said I'd find it with you, Jem. I'll never stop being glad I listened to them. And with Margaret content with William, even though weavers have hit hard times and their wages are poorer, I expect 'tis a story she likes to tell, too.'

Leaning over the bed, she kissed each of the children, and then went out of the room.

A smile on his face, Jem followed his wife, his hands in his trouser pockets.

In the fingers of one of his hands, he clutched the chip of stone that he always kept with him - the chip he'd taken for luck from one of the Knights on the occasion when, ten years earlier, he'd slipped from the cover of the trees, run across to one of the stones, hidden behind it and waited to utter the words he'd wanted to come true more than anything else in the world from the moment he'd first set eyes on the girl in the green cotton calico dress.

SEVENTH HEAVEN

ROSIE ORR

The last hour or so had been a ruddy nightmare, thought the Departures Angel as he irritably tidied the brochures on the marble counter. All those French composers pushing and jostling, demanding Awaydays for Paris *absolument* effing *immédiatement*. Little Ravel had nearly got himself knocked over, and as for that Berlioz, if he spoke to him in that tone of voice next time... Sometimes he thought it was a mistake to let the Top Creatives nip back to Earth for a day once a century, he really did. Missed the racket and the filth and the how's-your-father and that - all essential to get the old creative juices flowing, apparently. Paradise just didn't light their fire, as that Goya kept spray painting all over the Boundary Walls...

Tsk! What a morning. The black and white marble floors had been murder to polish, and the sodding saints' statues had taken forever to dust. Nearly eleven o'clock, thank Upstairs; time to turn the sign on the Departures Hall's great bronze doors to CLOSED.

He was drifting across the lobby, thinking what a load of cobblers *Symphonie Fantastique* was, when he heard heavy footsteps approaching on the gravel outside. Lumbering. Determined. Of a type that suggested their owner wouldn't take kindly to being denied service. With a sigh, he turned back to the counter.

Monet dumped his bulging canvas bag on the floor, shoved his battered straw hat to the back of his head and scowled. '*Merde*. Where's Kevin?'

'Kev's helping out with Arrivals today, sir, there's been a bit of an influx what with all these wars and that going on.'

He indicated the elaborate name badge pinned to his robe. 'Raymond, sir. And you would be…?'

'Monet, Claude. Normandy, if you please.'

'Ooh, I'm sorry,' managing to convey by his tone that he was not, 'I got nothing left for France. Just had a load of composers in, and before that it was Baudelaire and that crowd.'

Monet kicked his bag so hard it skidded across the floor and thrust his great head so close to Raymond's he could see the blackheads peppering the fleshy nose, the purple veins threading the sagging cheeks, the tangles in the straggling white beard. 'One more day surrounded by nothing but fluffy pink clouds and smirking cherubs - milk and honey for every meal and nothing but nectar - *nectar*!' he clutched at his throat, made a sort of gurgling noise, 'by way of *apéritif* and I swear I shall, shall…'

Raymond knew an emergency when he saw one. 'Don't take on, sir, I'm sure we can fit you in somewhere.' He turned to the celestial computer humming quietly behind him. 'Let's see.' He began to press keys, pull levers. 'Manet…Manet…'

The old man closed his eyes, shuddering. '*Monet*.' He spoke through gritted teeth.

'Gotcha. Just getting your details up…' A bell pinged, lights flashed on the console. 'Here we go.' Raymond bent closer to the screen, glowing now with a seemingly endless succession of ever more vibrant images. He gave a low whistle. 'Well get *you*. Love the pics - mm, specially those water lilies, *fabuloso*.' He frowned. 'So it's some sort of water venue you'd be after today, would that be right?'

'*Vraiment*, some tranquil river, or lake.'

'Plus it says here you're a…' he peered more closely at the screen, now showing a sumptuously laid table, '*bon viveur*. Right, you'll be wanting your tea thrown in, then. So what sort of nosh would you be looking for? Nice steak? Fries?'

'I used to particularly enjoy…'

'Don't tell me - *snails!*' He pretended to vomit. 'Am I right or am I right?'

The old man closed his eyes. 'A little duck pâté, to begin. Followed by Lobster Newburg, perhaps, or a dish of *Coquilles St Jacques Florentine*.' He sighed. 'And of course *Poulet au Champagne* was always a favourite - the sauce made with *Veuve Clicquot, naturellement*, and the finest *petits champignons*.'

'Oh dearie me. I'm afraid it's not going to be easy to find somewhere to suit.' He pulled more levers, pressed a small red button. After a moment, the screen went dark. 'Nothing left in Europe at all, Sir.' He peered at a tiny faded Union Flag that had appeared in the corner of the screen, pulsating excitedly. 'Ooh, I tell a lie. Plenty of passes left for England.'

Monet opened his eyes and glared at the Departures Angel. 'England? Ha! Don't speak of it! The *cochons* refused to hang my paintings in the Academy Exhibition! As for the food... the weather...'

Snatching up his bag, he turned to go.

Raymond touched the Union Flag on the screen, blinked as a series of stunning images flashed up in quick succession. 'Mr Manet?'

The old man wheeled round, snarling. '*Monet*.'

'Ask me we got something that'll def hit the spot up Oxfordshire, *mon brave*. Fancy gardens, top o' the range nosh. Very nice. Very nice indeed.'

'But where exactly...?'

Raymond put a finger to his lips. 'That's for me to know and you to find out, *sir*. Ready to go?'

'I...'

'Good call.' He rummaged under the counter and brought out two small phials, one red, one blue. He handed the old man the blue one. 'Right. Be back at the Pearly Gates by sunset. Swig this Speed o' Light Tincture down when it's time to return.' He passed over the red phial. 'Knock this one back now. Only got the Corporeal flavour left, I'm afraid.'

'Pardon?'

'Means people'll be able to see you. Don't draw attention is my advice.'

'I…'

'Hurry, if I was you, or it won't be worth bothering going; got your crayons and that?'

At the mention of crayons the old man's eyes lit up, looking so joyous Raymond wished he had an artistic bent himself, he really did. Beaming, Monet picked up his bag, uncorked the phial and drank. '*Alors, merci mon ami! À bientôt!*'

'Later…' Raymond waggled his fingers cheerfully. 'Don't do anything I wouldn't do…'

The sound of rushing winds, a burst of the Heavenly Choirs screeching *Born to be Wild*, and Monet vanished.

At first there was the sound of birds singing, water trickling, then the lemon tang of ferns and grasses, the moss-green scent of water. He opened his eyes.

He was standing on a narrow path, the ground soft beneath his boots. Overhead the sky was a rinsed blue; shafts of sunlight pierced the branches of the trees. Rocks and boulders bordered the path, which followed - *best, oh best of all!* - a small pond, a deeper blue sky of positively sublime richness contained in its still reflection. And on the opposite bank - *surely he was dreaming?* - stood a tiny thatched Japanese tea house, a hint of pink amidst the smooth teak wood lines of the verandah, a sliver of a *tatami* mat just visible through the open door, surrounded by a profusion of manicured shrubs: miniature pine and box trees, a profusion of bamboo, each containing a thousand shades of green and yellow. And then there was the rockery, a pair of bronze herons poised to take flight, a stone lantern set deep in a recess…

A tear trickled down his cheek. It was as if he had returned home.

A sudden breeze rattled the slender branches of a nearby ash tree, changing the light entirely, deepening the shadows and dappling the surface of the pond with coins of silver. Quickly he pulled a folding stool from the depths of his bag, set paints and brushes and linseed oil on a nearby rock, placed a small canvas in readiness. He would look and look until he *saw* - and then he would begin.

The sun was considerably lower in the sky when he came to himself again. The canvas, now completed, was an explosion of colour: luminous layers of paint, here blending, there overlaying, now scraped down with the finest of palette knives - broad brushstrokes, vertical brushstrokes, dappled brushstrokes defining sky, water, vegetation. And at the centre of the painting, its heart, the serene, reflective waters of the pond.

Painfully he got to his feet. His back ached, his reddened eyes watered and stung. Lifting his hat, he scratched at his scalp, regarded the canvas before him. Smiled very slightly. Finished? No painting was ever finished, but at least he had managed to set down a little of what he felt…

His stomach rumbled. Apparently there would be food. Excellent. Quickly he cleaned his brushes and secured the canvas to the side of his bag. After a last affectionate look at the scene, the waters of the pond now a deep ultramarine, he set off down the path.

Soon he came to a wooden bridge over a stream, and went on past another pond, larger, this time, planted with a great drift of bulrushes. Exquisitely tended gardens lay ahead; he would have given much to explore them, but his stomach was rumbling more insistently now, and in the distance he see could a gabled roof soaring above a high stone wall, with a flight of steps leading to an archway.

'…*you'll be wanting your tea thrown in, then…*'

Might this not be a restaurant?

He hurried on breathless, lumbered up the steps, through the archway and stopped dead.

A terrace set with little tables lay before him. Smiling couples sipped at cocktails, toyed with canapés. Beyond the terrace was a most elegantly proportioned dining room; tantalising aromas wafted through the open glass door. As if in a trance, Monet moved towards it.

'*Monsieur*? May I be of assistance? You have booked a table?'

A young man, clearly a waiter, blocked his path, looking anxious as he registered the battered straw hat, the great tangle of beard, the stained and creased linen jacket.

Monet frowned. He could smell *langoustines*, if he was not mistaken, and he wanted some. *Now*. He shifted his bag to the other hand. Scowled. 'Raymond sent me.'

The waiter's eyes widened; he bowed. 'Of course, sir.' He gulped. He'd only been in the job a month; wouldn't do to screw up now. The old guy must be some great writer, or composer or something; some of the wealthiest, most famous guests often looked, quite frankly, like vagrants. 'Welcome to The Orangery, sir. Allow me to show you to a table.'

Monet inclined his head graciously, admiring the delightfully airy space, the white linen table cloths, the tall white candles, the gleaming wine glasses. Once settled, with his bag (damp and stained now with mud and oil paint) dumped on the elegantly upholstered chair beside him - the waiter opened his mouth to remonstrate, thought better of it - he perused the proffered menu. *Le Manoir aux Quat' Saisons, Raymond Blanc*, eh? French, thank God.

'An *apéritif*, perhaps, sir?'

Monet had a brief but distressing memory of crystal chalices brimming with nectar. 'Calvados. *Grande, naturellement.*'

'Certainly, sir. Perhaps when I return I may take your order? As you see, we have the Five Course menu, always very popular.'

Monet shook his head. The Seven Course menu began with a roasted pumpkin soup, featured seared *langoustines*, Cornish brill, and Aberdeen Angus beef in a red wine *jus*. It ended with banana and passion fruit sorbet and chocolate mousse with almond milk ice-cream. Monet tapped the bottom of the page, where a cheese course was listed as a possible extra.

'The Seven Course, sir, naturally. With cheese.' Christ, the old boy would be lucky if he didn't drop dead on the spot; he'd barely managed to cram his bulk into his chair as it was. 'An excellent choice, sir. I will send the *sommelier* to discuss your choice of wines.' As he turned away, he caught sight of the painting secured to the side of the bag and stood gazing, transfixed. '*Wow*. I mean… bloody 'ell, *wow*! That is just so… so…' He shook his head, peered more closely. 'But how…?'

Monet looked up from the wine list. He shrugged. 'Here a little square of blue… an oblong of pink… a streak of yellow…' He returned to the wine list. '*Alors*, my Calvados if you please. '

'At once, sir.'

With a bow, the waiter hurried away.

Later - much later - Monet popped the last morsel of *Brie de Meaux* in his mouth and washed it down with the remains of his second bottle of *Nuits-Saint-Georges 1er Cru 2010*. As he brushed ineffectively at the debris lodged in his beard the waiter reappeared, looking nervous. 'May I enquire if everything was to your satisfaction, sir?'

'Satisfaction?' The old man closed his eyes, folded his hands over his enormous belly and gave an enormous sigh. 'Hardly…'

The waiter froze.

A smile spread over Monet's face. '*Mon ami*, it was *superbe*. I have been in seventh heaven.'

By the time Monet had been helped out to the terrace, where he insisted on sitting for a moment to admire the sunset flaring amongst the trees in a riot of brilliant scarlet and orange, it was long past the end of the waiter's shift. He could only imagine what the old man was seeing with his rheumy, bloodshot eyes, and resolved to bring him a small brandy to aid his enjoyment; on his way home he would call in at reception to enquire the identity of their guest. With a bow, he departed.

After a moment Monet extricated the little blue phial from his pocket, turning it this way and that in the fading light, admiring the fleeting iridescent colours…

It was a few minutes before the waiter could fulfil his errand; a little silverware remained to be cleared, the sommelier had a new joke to relate as he polished a snifter, added a generous measure of marc and set it on a gleaming salver.

At last, Monet raised the phial to his lips.
…the sound of rushing winds, a burst of the Heavenly Choirs warbling Homeward Bound…

When the waiter returned, the terrace was empty; a light breeze had sprung up, pinkish clouds begun to drift across the moon. He was about to turn away when he paused, astonished. Propped on the table was the exquisite little painting that had enthralled him earlier, its colours luminous in the deepening twilight.

Beside it was a scrap of paper, with the single word '*Merci*'.

THE VEGETARIAN DOG

ANDREW PUCKETT

In the shallow valley of the upper Thames west of Oxford lies some of the most remote countryside in Southern England. It's remote because it's generally rather flat, marshy in parts, and there aren't many roads. But it's genuinely unspoilt, there are roe-deer, hare - and curlew still come up from the coast and nest there in summer. It's not chocolate box, contains real locals and there's even cow-dung on some of the roads which is certainly *verboten* in the choc box villages of the Cotswolds and Chilterns. It's here my parents moved around 1970 after they left farming - or rather, farming left them.

We knew all about cow-dung on the roads when we still had the farm. A housing estate had grown up around the farmyard which was separate from most of the fields, so that the cows had to walk along the road to be milked. And the people who moved into the houses complained about it. The thing is, as my father tried to explain to them, when cows walk from grass onto tarmac, the extra jolting makes them… well, loosen up. As he said, how do you potty train a cow? And they were there first, weren't they?

Anyway, my father found other employment and he and my mother rented a 400 year old cottage about fifteen miles from Oxford as the crow flies, although further by road - and further still by river. It was owned by an airline pilot who worked abroad and it was large enough to be divided in two. We lived in the larger part, while the smaller was taken by a succession of tenants, some nice, some not so and some downright odd. There was quite a turnover, so maybe it was us who were odd.

But I have one particular couple in mind, Paul and Susan.

They were ultra-strict vegans: no eggs, no milk, no leather shoes or belts - nothing that was of animal origin. And this was in the days before quorn, so it was that much more difficult. Paul was tallish and thin and always had an eager to please expression - these days we would call him geekish. He was a doctor of chemistry who worked in the Radcliffe where I was also working at the time. His wife, Susan, was shorter, slightly plump in both body and face and always wore a sincere expression. Her voice was soft, slow and very earnest. She stayed at home. There were no children, but they did have a dog, a vegetarian dog.

It was a spaniel and was allowed to eat only cheese. Well, I'm sure they would have given it salad if it would have eaten it, but dogs tend not to like salad. It was thin, didn't look very happy and spent its time slinking around with a puzzled look on its face as though trying to solve some great mystery.

Now, I have some sympathy with vegetarians and don't eat any red meat myself these days. Back then, I had the idea that if I wanted to eat meat, then, morally, I should be prepared to kill the animal myself. So I used to take the shotgun and look for rabbits and pigeons. Unfortunately, I'm a lousy shot, so I didn't get to eat much meat. I remember once returning with a rabbit, and my father staring at it in amazement.

'My God,' he said, "that must be the unluckiest rabbit in Oxfordshire! To be in your sights and actually get hit…'

Now, humans can be vegetarians and perfectly healthy with it, but dogs are natural carnivores and to deny one meat is… well, cruel. But maybe Susan and Paul didn't know that.

Susan's concern for the welfare of animals was extensive and included those that the local farmer put in the fields surrounding the cottage - sheep, cattle and sometimes a horse or two.

They worried about the horses in particular, especially the effect the rain might be having on their health, so they purchased and rigged up a tarpaulin between the trees that grew beside the stream for them to shelter under. The horses showed no interest in it whatever, so when it rained, Paul and Susan tried to herd them underneath it, so that they could appreciate the benefits. I'm sorry to report that they didn't; no sooner had the horses been herded under it, they came out again. At first, they just shot out of the other side, so Paul and Susan made sure that one of them was at each end, but to no avail. The horses would turn quickly and gallop past their outstretched arms.

It was the same when they tried it with the sheep. Sheep will shelter behind a wall, but they didn't like the tarp. Maybe it was the flapping in the wind, maybe it just didn't seem as reliable as a stone wall. For whatever reason, they didn't like it. The cattle had long, curved horns, and wisely perhaps, Susan and John left them alone. Eventually, the tarp filled with water and collapsed.

Oh, I'd nearly forgotten the snails. They put a notice up in the shared doorway that we were to watch out for snails so that we could avoid treading on them. Difficult in the dark, particularly so after a visit to The Dun Cow in Northmoor, a joyous survival from the thirties. (Gone now, sadly. The brewery in Abingdon opted to take shelter under the Whitbread umbrella – and was shut.)

Anyway, my sister, heartless teenager, used to collect empty snail shells, take them to the doorway and make ostentatious crunching noises with them.

At this time, all the family were living there: my sister back from agricultural college in Leicester, my brother from Porton Down where he'd been working and me back from London. By and large, we all got on.

One Sunday, my mother was cooking lunch and I was gazing idly out of the small kitchen window. A rat appeared on the lawn, scampering from left to right. A minute or so later, it crossed again, from right to left. And then again. I don't know why. It was a large, fully grown rat.

I called out to my father who was in the sitting-room. 'Hey, there's a rat here, just running to and fro - look...'

He came in and peered out of the window.

'So there is,' he said. 'Get the shotgun...'

Having grown up on a farm and worked one himself for a living, he detested rats and would go considerably out of his way to kill one.

Now, a rat can't help being a rat, it was born that way. But it's reckoned that they consume a fifth of the world's entire grain harvest. Twenty percent, which is enough to feed a lot of hungry people worldwide. The rat would doubtless retort that humans eat four fifths of the world's grain - enough to feed a lot of hungry rats.

But then again, the rats didn't sow or harvest the grain, we humans did, which we feel gives us some claim over it. Anyway, all farmers hate rats for the damage they do and all consider it their professional duty to kill them whenever the opportunity presents itself.

I handed him the shotgun. My mother said plaintively, 'Must you? In the kitchen? While I'm cooking lunch?'

My father said, 'Sorry, but a man's got to do...'

He very gently eased the casement open, then raised the gun to his shoulder and waited, still as a statue. Mother sank resignedly into a chair with her eyes shut and hands over her ears. A minute passed... then the rat, oblivious, scampered across the lawn again.

BOOM... The kitchen filled with noise and smoke.

'Got him,' I heard dimly, my hearing stunned by the noise.

I ran outside and searched the lawn. No rat.

'No you didn't, you missed,' I called out. 'Silly old fool,' I added, but *sotto voce*.

'I did NOT miss,' came back through the window. And there's no doubt that, unlike me, my father was a very good shot. One of the last things he did in his life was to kill a fox (it had been killing mother's chickens) with one shot from a

.410 shotgun, no easy feat.

I continued searching and was at last rewarded. The rat had been blasted onto the flower bed.

'Here it is,' I called, and flicked it onto the lawn with a stick.

From out of nowhere came the vegetarian dog, seized the dead rat, and made off with it...

I wish I could tell you what happened next, but I can't, because I don't know.

Did the vegetarian dog go back to Susan and John to show them what it had caught? 'Master, mistress, look - *this* is the answer to the mystery, *this* is what I like. May I have some more, please?'

Or did it, knowing its owners, take its prey to some hidden corner and consume it in secret?

I can't help thinking that if it was the former, we might have heard something. Susan would have let out a shriek and/or we'd have had a complaint about the sullying of their dog. Maybe they were out at the time, but in that case, why was the dog loose?

They left the cottage not long afterwards, so we never knew for sure what happened to the rat remains, except that some instinct assures me, it ended up in the vegetarian dog's stomach!

TO HADES VIA CARFAX

RADMILA MAY

This story is very loosely based on the story from Greek and Roman mythology of the musician Orpheus's journey to the Underworld to rescue his wife Eurydice from Pluto, the King of Hades.

That night there was a good crowd in The Olde Ratte of Oxford Tavern. No, I won't tell you where The Olde Ratte is in case them Oxford City Council rat catchers get to hear, know what I mean? Anyhow I swaggers up to the bar and shouts out, 'Drinks on me, boys.'

'You're in a good mood,' someone calls.

'I've a right to be. Wait till you hear where I've been and what I've been up to.'

'Something dodgy, I'll be bound,' someone else shouts.

'What do you mean, dodgy? I'm legit, always have been. Anyhow, got me own business now. *Stuart Services,* that's what I am. And before you ask, why Stuart, it's a ana - ana - ana - whatsit of Rattus, that's Latin for Rat which is what I am and so are the rest of you. I do jobs for people what ask me to do jobs for them.'

'Get a move on, will you?'

'All right then, pin your ears back, and listen. I was in my office, yeah, I got an office now, and a computer and all that stuff. And in comes this mouse, tittupping around like mice do. Don't that get on your wick? Does mine. She, I reckon she was a she 'cos she had this straw hat with flowers all over - was waving a white hankie or something.

'I come with a flag of truce,' she says in a little mincing voice.

I just looks at her.

'I have come on a mission. I have been sent by Jack Orfey. Of course, you will know who I mean.'

I waits and she goes on, 'Jack Orfey, the singer. He has a mission for you.'

'Paid, I hope. I'm running a business not a charity. So what is this mission?'

'His wife's been abducted. By Pluto.'

'You mean the dog off the cartoon?'

She fairly snaps my head off. 'Of course not. I'm talking about Pluto. Lord of the Underworld, you ignoramus. I am the Sibble.' Leastways I think that's she said. All Greek to me.'

'What the hell's a - a - what you said?'

All of a sudden her voice changes. 'How the heck should I know, you stupid git? I'm just doing what I'm told. And you better too. Or it'll be the worse for you.'

'Who says?'

'Jack says. He's got powerful friends, know what I mean?'

Not for sure, but I can guess. There are some people you don't want to mess with, not if you want to stay in business. So I nods.

'What I got to do?'

'Rescue his missus from Lord Pluto.'

'You mean go into the Underworld? If that's just the sewers under Oxford, that's a doddle. I knows them pretty well.'

'Nope. The Underworld is under the sewers. Way under.'

'And how do I get there?'

She looks over her shoulder, all nervous-like. 'Pluto mustn't get to know you're coming. Or why,' she whispers.

'So where do I start?'

'You know the big postbox at Carfax? Be there by midnight. When the clock strikes rap on the side and a door will open.'

And with that she's gone. Nothing to show she's been there but then on top of the printer I sees something gleaming. A gold coin. And where there's one I reckon there'll be more to follow. And I'd be a mug to pass that up, wouldn't I?

So there I am at Carfax just before midnight. All around me is crowds, mostly drunk, staggering all over the Cornmarket and up and down the High Street. And there's street musicians and that, strumming away on their so-called musical instruments and bawling their heads off. Huh! Call that music? No way. Horrible racket, is what I call it. Didn't ought to be allowed. But that's as may be. And they don't half make a mess but that's no bad thing what with the takeaway food they drops. All over the place so I did get a nice bit of hamburger to chew on my way to that postbox.

And there it was, just where the four roads meet. But no sign of a door. So I waits and when I hears midnight strike I raps on the side of the post box and sure enough there's a door. It opens and a voice says, 'Come along, come along, I ain't got all night.'

It's her. The Sibble. So in I hops and there she is. She grabs me arm with her little mouse paws and we fall and fall down a cliff for what seems like hours. Down, down, down into the blackest dark you ever did see. And then all of a sudden we're on our feet with a wood all around us, not that we can see much, it being so dark everywhere.

'This way,' she says. 'I know where we can get a light.' So I follows her and - what do you know, there's a faint light in the distance. We gets nearer and it's a tree with one bright shiny gold-coloured branch.

'Go on, take it.'

'Will it burn me?'

'Don't be daft. Just get a move on.'

So I yanks at it. At first it won't come, in fact it lets out a squawk. But then it does. Not the whole branch, just a twig. But there's enough to see by. Just.

We take a path between the trees. And then we comes to a table all spread out with food. Well, I'm not one to pass up a free nosh. Would you? But just as I'm tucking in some hens come rushing out from between the trees. And these hens are big girls, with huge sharp beaks, not the sort you'd want to upset.

'Who are you?' I says.

'I'm a Narpy,' one of them says. 'And my friends, they're Narpies too. Both of 'em.'

'What's a Narpy?'

But I never do find out because all of a sudden I hears a howling in the distance. A dog howling. Coming nearer and nearer. Then I sees it and, blow me, it's a dog with three heads. A dog with one head's dodgy enough, dogs not being friends to rats. Three is very, very bad news.

So we scarpers, me and the mouse. Holding paws, would you believe?

After a while, we comes to a river, all black and smelly and a right old torrent as well. Fair flooding, it was. And in the middle of the river there's a rowing boat with an old man at the oars pulling towards the other bank.

Well, that dog's getting closer and closer. So, no hanging about.

'Oy, come back,' I shouts.

'Got yer coin?' he shouts back.

As luck would have it, I have got a coin. That gold job what the Sibble gave me. So I waves it at him. 'That do?'

He's back across the water like greased lightning.

'One coin, one passenger.'

'What about little me?' says the Sibble.

'Another trip, another coin. Unless the dog gets her first,' he adds, smirking.

That gets me, so it does. I ain't no friend to mice, but I reckons it hard to leave her behind. I waves the coin again. 'Gold, this is. Worth a lot.' Well, I guess I can get it back on expenses. 'Enough for the two of us.'

'All right, both of you. Hop in, darl.' And I have to say,

taking her with me was one of the best days' work I ever did, though she got up my nose no end.

So we both hops in. Close up, the old man's horrible. Being a rat, I'm used to filth although my dear old mum keeps our abode in Parktown as clean as you can keep anything in a sewer clean. But he was something else. Flies, maggots, God-knows-what, crawling out of his beard all over him. And the pong. Fair turned my stomach.

When we gets to the other bank, he dumps us. 'Be off with you. I ain't expecting you back.' And he laughs like a drain. As if he knew something we didn't.

All around us there's a dark and shadowy space. Can't see much but with that golden twig, there's a path ahead just visible, all stones and potholes but a path nonetheless with rocks and boulders all around. And ahead there's a cliff with a big black hole. The entrance to a cave. But it's the only way to go. So me and the mouse takes a deep breath and plunges right in.

Thirsty work, all this talking... 'Thanks, mate, I'll have another of the same.'

Them caves, they was something, I'm telling you. Sometimes we squeezed down a narrow passage way, sometimes we came out into a huge cavern. And there were pictures on the walls. Big animals like elephants, other big animals which could have been bulls and huge cats with enormous teeth. 'Mammoths, bison, sabre-tooth tigers,' murmurs the mouse. Little show-off. But I nods as if I'd known all the time. Nothing to be seen though, even with the golden twig.

And the furthest cave is a huge room with desks in it. And a load of young people all in white and black, all weeping and sobbing fit to bust. I knows who they are, they're them undergrads what are taking exams, poor little sods. Funny thing, though, they're transparent. Like ghosts.

At the back of the room there's two thrones. One of them,

a right big job with rubies and diamonds and emeralds all over, is empty. The other isn't. On it is a woman all in black and covered in more jewels.

'The Queen of Hades,' whispers the mouse, and some name I didn't catch. But I knows her by another name. Rodelinda. Or Rodent Linda. And I knows her. She is one scary dame. Not someone to cross with. Not if you value your meat-and-two-veg.

But I pretends I never seen her in all my natural. I bows very, very low. 'Mighty queen. We are in search of - of - Blow me, what's the girl's name?'

Just in time, the mouse pipes up, 'Dissie. Wife of Jack Orfey. He wants her back. He'll pay good money for her.' Daft name, if you ask me, but maybe it's short for something longer.

Rodelinda's eyes light up but she don't speak.

'So can we go get her?' I says. 'Please,' I adds.

Then she says, 'Yes, you bleeding well can. I'm right pissed off with the little cow. I had a good pitch here until she turned up and queered it. Little tart.'

She gets off her throne and beckons us to a door at one side of the cave. She opens it and goes through. We follows.

And instead of more gloomy caves and stuff there's a walled garden what I recognise. Sort of. Like the Botanic Gardens, you know, down the bottom of the High Street. But different, sort of back to front. And in the middle there's another of them thrones, also empty, and in front of the throne there's this young woman with golden curls and big blue eyes. Bit pudgy, though.

Ignoring that, I calls out, 'Are you Dissie? Wife of Jack Orfey?'

She twirls round and calls out, 'Who are you?'

'I'm your hubby's messenger. And I've come to rescue you and take you home to hubby.'

She opens those big blue eyes. 'Rescue? Oh, that's like

totes mega-cool. Is that, like, just for the day? That would be so-o-o-o-o awesome.'

'Where's Him?' whispers the mouse.

'You mean the God Pluto?'

Dissie simpers. 'He's just gone behind a bush. You know, to have a -'

'You mean to have a slash,' says Rodelinda. 'His age, he has them all the time. Stop rabbiting and get a move on. You're going home permanent.'

'OMG, no,' says Dissie. 'I won't.' And she stamps her foot.

'You useless little trust fund princess, you're just out for what you can get,' snarls Rodelinda. 'You're going back where you belong, you little gold-digger. You behave yourself or you'll be brown bread.'

'You'll be WATF, you just wait and see. IKR, Pluto, he's like my BFF, you old slag. Soz, fashwise, you're totes last year.'

And the two of them are at it hammer and tongs. I will say for Dissie, she can give as good as she gets, even if I can't understand the half of it due to her talking in text-speak.

But after a while, I can see the bushes shaking and a big man with an even bigger beard coming out. He sees us and shouts, 'What the Almighty F***'s going on?'

Time to go. So I grabs one of Dissie's hands and Rodelinda grabs the other and we're off, with little Sibble tagging along behind. But we're not making good time, and I keeps thinking about that dog, the one with three heads. So I says to Rodelinda, 'What do we do now?'

'Wait a moment,' she says. But there's Pluto shouting at us and Dissie tugging at my hand trying to get away and moaning about how we're all so mean, why can't we treat her like a grown woman and why can't she go back to the only man she could ever love? As if!

'Shuddup,' shouts Rodelinda. 'You're just his little bit on the side.' She puts her hand to her mouth and does a sort of yodel. And all of a sudden there's a load of noise, roaring and yowling and miaowling. Cats. Big cats, little cats and all sizes in between.

'Oh,' says Dissie. 'What dear little pussy cats. Puss, puss, come here.'

But the Sibble is in a bad way. 'Help,' she whimpers. 'It's the Furries.' Not surprising she's upset when you think that if there's one thing cats like more than anything else it's a nice tasty mouse. Of course, that's just for the normal house cats but they was only part of the crowd. The big ones, lions and tigers and such, they was more interested in Dissie, particularly if she was stupid enough to try and cuddle them. She might too, her being clearly a born idiot.

At the moment though, there's a bit of a standoff between the cats and the three-headed dog and some mates of the dog that have just turned up. That's a relief, I can tell you. But I reckons that whichever one wins out will be looking at us. So, no hanging around.

And that's what Rodelinda reckons too. 'Go,' she says. 'Go now.'

But Dissie hangs back. 'I want to go back to King Pluto. I don't care what you say, he was good to me. He said I was his little cuddlekins.'

'Little cuddlekins, my backside,' snaps Rodelinda. 'If you don't go now, right now, I'll set the cats on you. Nothing they like better than a dumb blonde.'

No arguing with that. Not even for Dissie. So we're off again, me dragging Dissie along, teetering on her high heels, and the Sibble on my shoulder. Gor, what a menagerie. When we gets to the river, there's that dirty old ferryman in his boat pulled up to the bank.

'You again,' he says. 'If you're thinking of cadging a lift, think again.'

Only one thing for it. I lets go of Dissie, and lands a good left hook on his nose, and over the side he goes, straight into the water. Don't come up again, neither. Then I grabs Dissie's hand and pulls her in plus the Sibble and I rows - don't ask me how, for I ain't never rowed in my life, nor ever will again if I have anything to do with it - to the far side. And there's no going back because on the side we just came from there's hordes of cats, prowling up and down. And in the distance, dogs howling. I can take a hint. So could Dissie, just about.

Back again through that wood, double fast. And up the cliff what we had fallen down when we came. And then there's the door. And one last problem. No handle on this side, and no other way of opening it. And the howling sounds nearer. Like them dogs had got across the river.

I pulls the Sibble off my shoulder and throws her onto the ground. 'You got us into this mess,' I says. 'Now you get us out of it.'

She looks at me as if I was an idiot. 'Course I can,' she says, all light and airy. She knocks on the door, three times and then three times again. From the other side there comes a faint squeaking. She squeaks back. More squeaking. Then slowly, slowly, the door opens just a tad. A little paw appears. I put my shoulder to the door and it opens some more, then more again. Enough for me and more than enough for the Sibble. Bit of a tight squeeze for Little Miss Pudgy, but what with me and the Sibble pushing from the back and a whole tribe of mice what I'd never set eyes on before pulling from the front and, boy, was I glad to see them, we got her through. And all of a sudden we're all out and back outside that postbox on Carfax corner just as if we'd never been away. And there's Dissie's hubby, all smiles and hugs for his wee wifie. Stupid git, he never guessed she wanted to stay behind with Pluto. Not much of a thanks to me for all the danger I've been in, all to save that stupid little cow as didn't want to be saved. Not much for the Sibble either. But she did come by my office the next morning and leave a couple of gold coins. Which is how I'm here, boys, and standing a few rounds to all of you.

Was there anything else I learned from that trip to the Underworld? Well, first of all, there really is an Underworld. Right down, far, far below Oxford and all them old buildings. And you can get to it if you dig deep enough although, myself, I wouldn't advise it. As for Rodelinda, I daresay she'll pop up in the world above sometime. Wouldn't surprise me at all. Just give her a wide berth, that's all. Oh, and I've still got that gold twig. I gave it to my dear old mum and she put it in a glass vase what looks like a slipper. Lights up our little Parktown home so it looks quite classy. So maybe it was worth it. Maybe.

Explanatory Notes

Hades - *the Underworld*
The Sibble - *the prophetess Sybil who foretold the future*
Pluto - *King of the Underworld*
Jack Orfey - *Orpheus, an outstanding musician*
Dissie - *Eurydice, wife of Orpheus*
Narpies - *Harpies, terrifying monsters, half-women, half-birds, who tore their victims to pieces*
Furries - *the Furies, who pursued wrongdoers remorselessly*

The river is the River Acheron, a black torrent which all had to cross before reaching Hades, so swift that no one could do so except in a boat rowed by the boatman Charon. The three-headed dog is Cerberus who guarded the gates of Hades. However, the painted tunnels through which the rat and the Sibble pass are based on the painted prehistoric caves of the Dordogne while the Examination Schools and the Botanic Gardens are from present-day Oxford.

Rodelinda is the title of an opera by the composer Handel. Fortuitously it could easily be derived from the word Rodent and the name Linda – apt!

Textspeak: *OMG - Oh my God; totes - totally; WATF - Well And Truly F****d; IKR - I Know, Right; BFF - Best Forever Friend; soz - seriously*

THE WOODCUT

*A Ghost Story
in the manner of M. R. James*

PAUL W. NASH

Some years ago, at Oxford, a middle-aged librarian was asked to examine 'a few old books' which a friend's mother had been left by a distant relative, to see if there might be anything of value among them. Such requests filled the librarian - let us call him Edward Bliss - with a certain despondency. The 'old' books would usually turn out to be a shelf or two of recent novels and a family bible of the latter part of the previous century. However, there was always the possibility of something unusual coming to light, so Bliss accepted the invitation and walked to the house in North Oxford.

The library was a large room on the ground floor, piled high with books. It had a pleasing, slightly bitter smell of damp leather and paper which, together with the look of the place, gave Bliss a little optimism. There might, after all, be something worth finding here. He began to examine the books. Many contained the small label of William De Roche, the late owner of the house. The books were mostly of the later eighteenth and nineteenth centuries and, Bliss soon found, in very poor state.

However, one volume quickly caught his eye. It was bound in dark brown leather and showed blind-tooling on the spine, suggestive of the later sixteenth century. It was a small folio, about eleven inches tall, and stood at the end of a shelf of odd volumes of Victorian periodicals. Bliss drew it out, and was instantly disappointed for he knew from its weight that the binding was empty. The boards were of wood with bevelled edges, and covered with the same dark, blind-tooled leather he had observed on the spine. But the textblock had been removed.

The end leaves were, however, of some interest. The front pastedown bore an engraved armorial bookplate, probably of the first half of the eighteenth century. The pastedown on the back board was still more interesting. It had evidently been disturbed, and just visible along the foot was a strip of vellum with some black marks upon it. Clearly some manuscript, or perhaps an early printed sheet, had been used to line the board. Loosely inserted between the boards was the bookseller's receipt for the binding; when Bliss glanced at this, he saw the name of a local dealer and the very paltry sum which De Roche had paid. Aware that great treasures have been found beneath the end leaves of unremarkable books, Bliss put the binding aside and continued with his survey.

He was obliged to make a disappointing report to his friend. His mother's inheritance of books was of no great value. Bliss's friend looked downhearted, but thanked him warmly and asked if he would like anything from the library as payment for his labours. There was but one item in the collection he craved.

'But it is not even a book,' said his friend, when Bliss showed him the binding. 'It is just a cover. Would you not rather have something else?'

'Not at all. This binding pleases me very much.' And so he took the thing away, intending to examine it at his leisure.

Edward Bliss lived in rooms to the east of Oxford which he shared with his only companion, a brindled cat named Montague (after one of the great benefactors of his library). He had spent all day at the house of William De Roche, and when he arrived at his rooms, with his treasure under his arm, he expected the usual affectionate welcome from the cat. But as soon as Montague saw him, he leapt up from the cushions of the armchair and crouched upon the antimacassar, his ears back and eyes flaming.

'It's only me, old chap,' said Bliss. But Montague would not be calmed. He hissed. His tail bristled. He arched his back and stared at Bliss as if he were the fiercest dog or feline rival. But was he looking at Bliss? There was something in the way Montague moved his head that suggested he was regarding someone, or something, over Bliss's right shoulder. He spun round and had the fleeting sense of something dark that hurried from before his sight like a shadow before the sun. Indeed, he thought, it must have been a shadow cast by the shifting light from the street. He looked back at Montague, who seemed now ready to fight or flee. Bliss had never seen the creature look so large and wild. The cat clung for a moment to the apex of the chair, every muscle tense, then leapt to the floor and raced past his master and through the open door behind him. That was the last Bliss saw of Montague that evening, for the cat could not be tempted in to supper, even by the smell of fish and the special call which Bliss used when there was a treat in his friend's dish.

When Bliss had dined, he decided to retire early and defer the pleasure of examining the binding to the following day, which was a Sunday. He could not persuade Montague to return to the house, so had to retire without his usual companion. He felt unsettled by Montague's curious behaviour, and checked the doors and windows twice before retiring. When the moment came to put out the light, though he felt ashamed, he could not quite bring himself to do it.

That night he was troubled by nightmares. He dreamed he was back in his childhood home, in the kitchen with his late father. He opened a drawer in the table to find an unusual knife, with a broad blade ground at an angle. It was very bright and worn by countless resharpenings. Bliss knew, with the certainty of the dreamer, that his father meant to take up the knife and do him harm. He looked up at the old man, and wondered that he had not noticed before how very tall and thin he had become. His face too was unfamiliar. Indeed, now he looked more closely, Bliss could see that this was not his father at all but some other man. His lower jaw was unusually narrow and jutted forward. His nose was long, and his hair and side-whiskers gave him a dog-like appearance. He snarled and reached for the knife. As he did so Bliss saw that his left ear was hairy and pointed, and flattened against the side of his head.

He awoke and lay sweating for a time. Then he slept again and dreamed of a forest. It was dark and Bliss was an animal running through the undergrowth, fleeing from a huntsman. He could hear his pursuer's breathing close behind, and knew the hunter intended to kill and eat him if he could. Bliss ran on, but the way grew steeper until he was on a bank that was almost vertical. He struggled to ascend, through tangled creepers and clawed brambles, but could scarcely breathe with exhaustion and panic. Soon he could go no further and turned to look down at his pursuer, who was climbing inexorably through the web of branches. It was the same dog-faced man. He looked still more brutish now, with yellow teeth and eyes. His long, hairy ears twitched, and in his right hand he held the strange knife, which gleamed and glittered as he advanced.

Again Bliss woke. This time, however, he was aware that something was in the room with him. For many minutes he lay trying to master his breathing and the furious beating of his heart. He knew something was present, though he could not see it. The light was still burning, so it was not a question of his visitor hiding in the darkness. It was somehow hiding in the light. After a while Bliss became aware of a low sound, like the growling of a dog. He fancied some great animal might be lying on the carpet between the bed and the door, just out of sight. He would be able to see it if only he raised his head. But he did not dare. He looked at the clock. It was nearly dawn.

He lay motionless for what seemed like hours, until the sky was light. Then at last he pulled himself together, rose and examined the room. There was nothing to be seen. When he opened the door he found Montague curled up on the carpet in the corridor, though the creature fled again as soon as he saw his master.

With the sun shining and a simple breakfast inside him, Bliss began to feel a good deal better. He did his best to dismiss the terrors of the night as mere fancies, and determined to delay no longer his examination of the binding he had acquired the previous day. It lay on his desk, just where he had left it. The first thing he looked at was the receipt. He noticed for the first time, that the document was dated only two weeks previously. The binding must have been among the last items De Roche had acquired. Then he examined the bookplate. It showed a complex coat-of-arms. Bliss would need to consult certain reference works at the library to identify it, but he felt sure it must be the blazon of a gentleman-collector of the eighteenth century. Next he turned to the back pastedown. He gently picked at the corner of the paper and found it insecurely attached. A little careful work with a paper-knife soon allowed him to peel back the leaf, revealing what lay beneath.

His first emotion was disappointment. The vellum he had seen was the edge of a larger leaf, but the ink upon it was so faded and discoloured as to be scarcely legible. It appeared to be part of a deed or legal document, perhaps of the fifteenth century, but so little of the text remained that it was impossible to be sure. The leaf was very imperfectly attached to the board and Bliss was able to lift it to expose two further sheets of paper, clearly of much later date, which had been inserted behind the vellum. One was about the size of a picture-postcard and bore an impression, in brown ink, of a crude woodcut depicting a public hanging. Such woodcuts had been used and used again for two centuries to illustrate sensational broadsides and pamphlets describing executions, and were of no more than passing interest to the antiquary. The other sheet of paper had the pale blue-green tint of the last years of the eighteenth century. It was folded and bore a short manuscript in ink. Bliss held the paper to the light and read the date '1796' in the watermark. The handwriting, he thought, was very much in the style of that period. Then he read the text, which ran as follows:

I, John Dalton, printer of the City of Oxford, made this cut in the Year of Our Lord 1798 to present the Hanging of the notorious Murderer Samuel Sayers, who was held to have killed thirteen, five of them children and one an infant. I was at his Hanging in Oxford and saw the end of him. The crowd made a great noise for his death and, when it was done, came forward in large numbers and tore down his body and the gallows. Some Constables were able, by force, to take his body away for burial outside the City, but the people would not give up the gallows. A Carpenter had his saw, and cut the tree into many small pieces, which the people took away as tokens of the day. I paid two pennies for a piece of the old timber, and finding it to be good English beech, determined to make from it a Cut of the Hanging, of which I had made a sketch. This I did, at my Shop, and that same day printed a sheet describing the execution, which I sold for one halfpenny. Would to God I had not entertained such a conceit, for as soon as the cut was struck I was pursued by such a Demon that I could only think it the Spirit of the Murderer. I felt my life in peril, and begged the Reverend Cole to preserve me. He told me to consign to fire all the prints I had made save for one, and then to destroy the block. Thereafter I must pass the last print to another, who must take ownership of it, and so of the demon. I thought this most unjust, for why should I transmit the curse to another man as innocent as myself?

But the Reverend told me it must be so if I wished to be free. The demon cared not for justice and would pursue him that owned the woodcut, saint or sinner, till a means be found to cure it of its anger. I asked if I could not destroy the last print too, but the Reverend told me I should never be free if I did as much. With great labour, and some cost, I bought back all the sheets I had printed. When I had burned the prints and the block, I sat down to write these few words. I shall fix the last woodcut into the back of an old Erasmus which is to hand, and with it this account, and take the book to Parker who I hope may give a shilling for it.

Bliss read this singular testament twice. It recalled his fears of the night, though he was a rational man and told himself that such stories had power only over children and the simple-minded. Nevertheless, it would do no harm to research the story, in case it might throw light on the provenance of the curious binding. Bliss could do nothing until he returned to the library on Monday, however, so put the papers aside. As he went about the business of the day, the story occupied his mind in a most unhealthy manner, and when he lay down to sleep that night he was again prey to certain fancies and could not bring himself to douse the light. As he turned over in his bed, he wished he might be joined by Montague. But the cat had not been seen since that morning.

Bliss did not sleep. At dawn he rose, with heavy eyes, aching neck and the perfect conviction that something had spent the night in the room with him. Every tiny sound had made his heart race, though, in truth he had heard nothing which could not be numbered among the usual noises of the night.

After a meagre breakfast he departed for the library, taking the curious binding and its contents with him. After attending to his duties for several hours, Bliss found himself with time to begin his researches, and started by looking into the bookplate. It had, he discovered, belonged to Sir Roger Quinn, Bart (1762-1834), a minor diplomat who had amassed a large library at his country house in Gloucestershire. His books had been sold at auction after his death, and, with some effort, Bliss laid his hands upon the catalogue of the sale. Among the folio lots he found:

376 Erasmus, First Tome of the Paraphrase upon the Newe Testamente, *black letter, calf with blind tooling, London, E. Whitchurche,* 1548.
** Mark and Luke only. Rare edition with a good English binding.

It was the only folio by Erasmus in the catalogue, and thus Bliss thought the description likely applied to his binding. He cursed the unknown hand which had, at some date after 1834, extracted the printed leaves from their proper covering. Bliss could trace the ownership of the volume no further, so turned his attention to Dalton and his testament. He soon established that John Dalton the younger had been active as a printer and bookseller in Oxford between around 1770 and his death in 1808. More interesting, however, was the account of the trial and execution of Samuel Sayers, which Bliss found in Walton's *English trials, 1700-1840*.

Sayers had, it seemed, been a bookbinder, first at Lincoln and later at Oxford. A number of men, women and children had been discovered with their throats cut in both cities at the time of his residence. In some cases, the murderer had apparently devoured parts of his victims or had flayed them and taken away portions of their skin. Sayers was accused after several sheets of tanned hide which were believed to be human, were found in his bindery. In his kitchen were a number of small bones which a surgeon declared to have come from the foot and lower leg of a child. Sayers denied the charges, saying he had bought the skins from a travelling merchant, while the bones belonged to the foot of a pig. But the court had not believed him, and he was condemned to be hanged.

Walton repeated the story of the crowd tearing down the gallows and cutting it up for souvenirs, and added that it was reputed to have stood there for four hundred years before that day, and to have seen the death of more than a thousand unfortunates. He also mentioned the woodcut which was reputed to have been made from a piece of the gallows, and used to print a broadside account of the hanging, now lost. To Bliss, however, the most disturbing aspect of the account was the description of the criminal. Sayers was described as a tall, thin man with the face of a dog. His nickname among the locals had been 'Cur'.

Walton also noted that one man who had known Sayers swore he had seen him on the day after the hanging, striding along Market Street with a small and bloody knife in his hand, and many apparently believed the murderer's spirit had arisen to take revenge on his accusers.

This was all Bliss could discover of the story. But it was enough to make him wonder if there might not be, after all, forces and spirits abroad in the world about which rational men were, as yet, ignorant. And yet he could not bring himself to give up the woodcut, or the curious binding in which it had been hidden. They were valuable prizes for a bibliophile, especially since Bliss now had reason to think the woodcut unique. He pondered the question for the rest of the day and, by the time he left the library that evening, had quite convinced himself of one thing. If, he told himself, the spirit of Sayers had truly come to torment him, then his adversary was only a ghost, not a flesh-and-blood man who could hurt him. Sayers might haunt his dreams, or even his waking hours. But he could do no physical harm. If Bliss were steadfast and refused to fear the spirit, or the idea of the spirit, then it could have no power over him.

This belief was strengthened when he called upon the friend who had asked him to assess William De Roche's library, to enquire about the collector. He learned that De Roche had apparently died peacefully in his sleep, two days after the date of the receipt for the purchase of the binding.

When Bliss returned home there was still no sign of Montague. He was beginning to worry about his companion, for the cat had never before stayed away so long. However, as soon as he entered his small sitting-room, Bliss forgot about the creature. He found his desk disarranged, and the leather surface bore three long gashes, made with a sharp blade. There were further scratches on the paintwork, notably on the door. They were deep and curving, and at face-level - far too high to have been made by the claws of Montague. Bliss knew, with the same certainty he had felt in the dream of his father, that the spirit of Samuel Sayers had been at work, and that his knife was no mere gossamer, but a real blade that could cut through wood and leather.

At once he began to plan the disposal of the woodcut. He knew he could not simply discard or destroy it. He had to pass it on to someone who would take ownership of it willingly. He wondered about donating it, with or without the binding, to his library. But what would be the benefit of transferring the spirit from his home to his place of work? No. He had to find some way to get the woodcut far away, into unfamiliar hands. It was too late to visit any of the booksellers of Oxford that evening, but all the same, Bliss felt he had to act at once. He took out the woodcut and the manuscript account of its making, and fastened them in their original hiding place, behind the vellum leaf. Then he mixed flour and water and re-attached the pastedown leaving, as before, a thin margin of vellum visible. Without waiting for the paste to dry he took down his coat and went into the street with the binding in his hand. He would try the booksellers. Perhaps someone would be working late, or would answer his ring at such an

The Woodcut

hour.

As he hurried along High Street he saw something which made him change his plan. It was an old pedlar. Bliss knew the man by sight. He came to Oxford regularly, selling trinkets, jewellery and carvings from his tray. Bliss had once bought a brooch from him. Immediately he hailed the pedlar and offered him the curious binding.

'It is not my usual trade, sir,' he said.

'Perhaps not, but you could sell it on, I imagine, in the next town perhaps. I am in urgent need of a shilling. The binding is very old and worth much more than that. But if you will give me a shilling you may have it.'

The deal was struck and the object passed from one hand to another. The pedlar walked quickly away, and Bliss fancied a great weight lifted from his brow. Before returning to his rooms he stopped at Saint Mary's and dropped the shilling into the poor-box. He tried not to think of what it was he had transmitted to the pedlar, and through him to another. Bliss told himself he had been very fanciful, but had done the old pedlar a good turn, and someone, somewhere, would be glad indeed to add the curious binding to their library. He wondered if, when he next saw the pedlar, he would have the nerve to ask him what had become of the binding. But the question did not arise, for the old man was never again seen in Oxford, or in any other city that I know of.

When Bliss returned home he found the place perfectly peaceful. The presence he had sensed so recently was gone, and that night he slept soundly, troubled only by the usual dreams of a middle-aged librarian. After two days, Montague returned warily to the door. He sniffed into every corner, then spent two hours licking himself clean before settling down beside the fire. Later that evening, Bliss prepared a treat for him in the form of tinned mackerel and a very small dish of cream.

THE BLENHEIM DECEPTION
or WHAT YOU WILL

SYLVIA VETTA

'If music be the food of love, play on;
Give me excess of it, that surfeiting,
The appetite may sicken, and so die.'

A magical evening blesses a performance of the romantic comedy, *Twelfth Night*, in the great court of Blenheim Palace, part of the Arts Festival in honour of the 400th anniversary of the death of Shakespeare. A distinguished looking man of about fifty sits spellbound in the audience. His heart echoes the words of Shakespeare's lovesick Orsino, Duke of Illyria, whose words open the play. Heads turn away from the stage and towards the source of the melancholic sigh. Members of the audience whisper to each other as they recognise the smooth faced, handsome man in the front stalls as the opera director, Simon Lawrence, whose work is so highly regarded that he is known, in the world of music, simply as *the Duke*. With his large languid eyes, smooth complexion and long dark hair tied neatly at the nape of his neck, Simon the Duke, is instantly recognisable wherever he goes.

Seated in the row in front of him is Olivia Jenkinson, the soprano chosen for the lead role in the sensational new opera, *Double Jeopardy*, written especially for the finale of the Blenheim Festival. Simon Lawrence has come to observe the location. His intention is to begin the opera conventionally on the stage but he wants the final act to be performed by the lake into which Olivia will fling herself in a suicide bid, only to be rescued at the last moment by the hero.

Meanwhile, some ten miles away, in the little water-bound enclave known as Osney Island not far from Oxford Station, a young woman in her early twenties turns the key of the front door of a little terraced cottage overlooking the Thames. She has hardly stepped inside when a young man rushes towards her almost knocking her over. He laughs as he hugs her.

'Viola, I can't believe it. Look!' He points to his iPad. 'Peter Boteng is ill and he has recommended me to replace him at the Met. That means taking his place in the chorus and understudying Leporello; the Met have said 'yes' and I'm to fly to New York tomorrow!'

Singing *Madamina, il catalogo è questo*, Sebastian takes his sister in his arms and swings her around in the narrow hall until they fall back on the stairs in fits of laughter.

'Seb, that's marvelous! Can I come with you?'

In an instant the joy drains from her brother's face. He puts his face in his hands in despair.

'What's the matter? Seb, what's wrong?'

'Vi, I'm not thinking straight. I promised to start work at Blenheim next week. Remember?'

Viola did remember. After graduating from the Royal Academy of Music her brother had failed to secure a place in any of the, admittedly few, opera companies in the country and was consequently distraught. The disappointment was compounded by the need to earn money to pay off his student debts. His tutor, however, had found him a job of sorts, working back stage on the premier of the exciting new opera, *Double Jeopardy*. He would, at least, be in the opera world and who knows what might come of it? This had been Seb's thinking when he had eagerly accepted this non-singing job. He clenches his fists and bites his lips in desperation.

'I was hoping the Duke would notice me and give me the chance to join the chorus at the Coliseum next year. Now this offer,' said Sebastian pointing to his iPad. 'How can I turn down an opportunity like this? But the Duke will despise me if I drop out at the last minute. He'd never employ me again in any role whatsoever if I let him down now. Either way I'm damned. What can I do Vi?'

'Put the kettle on,' suggests his sister.

'Your answer to all problems - a cup of tea!' says Sebastian with the faint hint of a smile. But it is a good idea for as they brew the tea and start to drink, Viola finds time to think…

'Seb, you know I have three months of freedom before I start my post doc?' Seb nods.

'Why don't you let me help you. The Duke hasn't actually met you, has he? You told me he took you on the recommendation of your tutor, I've got that right haven't I?'

'Yes, but…' Sebastian rubs a hand over his lips, as he starts to read his sister's thoughts. Seeing brother and sister side by side it would not take a genius to work out that these two are twins. As so often happens in these cases brother and sister often 'read' each other's minds and Viola's, as yet unspoken, idea is not as outlandish to Seb as it might seem to others.

She goes upstairs and ten minutes later returns to the kitchen dressed in a pair of her brother's jeans and wearing his Greenpeace tee shirt.

'How have you managed to get into that?' he asks.

'It isn't comfortable but it's amazing what a tight bandage can do.'

'Your hair's a give-away.'

'I'm not going to leave it like this,' laughs Viola. 'Go and get the scissors and let's have a go at it. Don't worry, it'll grow again - go on!'

Sebastian is putting the finishing touches to Viola's new boyish coiffeur, when in walks his housemate, Harry.

'What are you two up to? Twins you may be but isn't this taking the symbiosis a bit far?'

Viola laughs at her fellow biologist's tease. 'Just you wait till you hear what we're planning to do…'

Thus, it happens that Viola - now answering to the name *Sebastian* - joins the crew at Blenheim while her brother heads for New York to grace the stage of the Metropolitan Opera House. Her appearance may have deceived the cast and crew but Viola's heart is still her own. She did not intend to fall in love with the Duke, who is more than twenty years older than her, but then, who deliberately falls in love? The Duke's eyes, however, are not focused on his young assistant, Sebastian: they caress Olivia, as he visualises himself as Richard Burton to her Elizabeth Taylor.

When he observes Olivia enjoying the company and jokes of the young Seb, an idea occurs to him. Instinctively he does not see Seb as a rival; indeed he has often seen such friendships spring up in the world of theatre. He seizes a moment alone with Seb and asks, 'Can I trust you? Can anything I say to you stay between us?' What could Viola say but 'Yes.'

During the rehearsals she becomes the director's personal envoy. He sends her to Olivia to sound out her feelings for him. The unfortunate Viola is in the invidious position of, in effect, having to woo another woman on his behalf. Back at home that evening she pours out her heart to Harry. 'She is lovely and he loves her but I can't do what he wants. I don't want her to love him. I want him to love me.'

Harry makes no comment but goes and puts the kettle on.

'I understand your tutor thinks highly of you, Sebastian,' said Olivia thoughtfully, one day. 'Why don't we try this duet together later on, when we have a break?' She had struggled in the early days of her own career and sympathises with a talented young music graduate having to work as a back-stage assistant. But Viola is all too aware that while she is identical in appearance with Sebastian, she certainly doesn't share his vocal chords. She hastily seeks to change the subject and takes the opportunity to pass on yet another message from the Duke. 'That's a wonderful idea,' she said, 'but the Duke wonders whether you might care to join him for lunch today. He said he doesn't mean a working lunch...'

Meanwhile in the pretty village of Woodstock a few hundred yards from the Palace, a certain Sir Andrew Cash checks in at The Feathers Hotel. The tall, awkward knight has an uncanny resemblance to the comic character in *Blackadder* and like that character, has more money than wit. He is accompanied by his friend, the baritone, Toby Wagstaff. The two men are joined by the feisty wardrobe mistress, Maria Perks. They eat drink and make merry at Sir Andrew's expense. Toby likes a little drink, and another, and yet another.

'To romansch,' Toby belches out the toast as he winks at Maria.

Malcolm Vole the producer is known, not for his sense of humour, but rather for his overbearing arrogance and self-absorption. Malcolm, in his own estimation is always right whether in his choice of bow-tie or in his judgment of other people, always quickly formed and thereafter invariable. The possibility of him being wrong is quite unthinkable. But, for once, he is about to see himself as others see him.

He walks into the green room just as the wardrobe mistress, Maria, is mimicking his plummy tones intimidating a lighting technician. A tipsy Toby nudges her aside. 'Allow me. The role of the producer of malware is perfect for me.' He pretends to adjust a bow-tie and glare over gold-rimmed glasses. But stumbling in on the scene, Malcolm is definitely not amused.

'You drunken idiots!' he storms. 'Have you no respect? If I have anything to do with it - and I do - you, Toby Wagstaff will never strut the professional stage again. You are a complete fool and you've ruined your voice with your over indulgence! As for you,' turning towards Maria, 'you little minx, wardrobe mistresses are ten a penny. I know just the right replacement for you.' With that he turns and strides away.

You might expect the terrible trio to be downhearted but, no... Maria is not just a pretty face. The wardrobe mistress knows the personal weaknesses of most of the cast and so she suggests a means to revenge themselves on Malcolm Vole.

'... and that vice means he will be susceptible, believe me,' she says. Sir Andrew and Toby grin and raise their glasses.

A little later Maria creeps into Olivia's dressing room while she is rehearsing on stage and picks up the star's mobile phone. She taps out a text message, then clicks on *send* and it wings its way through the ether to the phone of Malcolm Voles.

In the meantime, our heroine's problems are escalating. The Duke has noticed Sebastian's interest in him and has taken to giving him knowing smiles.

In a fit of distraction Viola has accidentally stumbled over a cleaner's full bucket of dirty water and soaked herself. In desperation she rings the ever faithful Harry and asks him to bring her a change of trousers and socks. 'I'll wait by the lake. But hurry, please hurry,' she pleads.

Harry makes haste but forty five minutes pass before Viola manages to get back to work.

'Where have you been?' demands an annoyed Malcolm Voles, but before Viola can answer, her inquisitor is distracted by a bleep on his phone. When he sees who has sent the message - Olivia - it receives his full attention: *'Even we special people need occasionally to let our hair down - it has been such a trying week. Tonight is the Son et Lumiere in the Marlborough Maze - everyone is coming cross-dressed in honour of Grayson Perry, the star guest for the evening. In case you don't recognise me, I am coming as a vicar. Will you indulge me and join the fun by coming as a lady of the night?*

Meet me in the middle of the maze at nine o'clock.'

Seeing that Malcolm is distracted, Viola slips away and turns the corner heading towards the water gardens but, on her way she collides with the Duke.

'Hey, slow down! I can think of a much better means of exercise on a sizzling day like this - How about skinny dipping in the lake? I'll meet you there as soon as the Palace closes to the public.'

As the Duke walks back to the set, he muses, 'Young Seb looked almost coy when I suggested the lake. What was Shakespeare's word for it? *Unmanned* – that was it. I wonder…? He has style and he's sensitive… mm.'

Viola paces up and down in the secret garden frantically wondering how to get out of this situation without offending the Duke. Her thoughts are interrupted by the bell, or rather the ping, of a text from her brother, which says he has been a success in New York, but Peter Boteng is now recovered and has resumed his role in the chorus and understudy. Sebastian is now on the last leg of his journey home to Oxford and is longing to hear his sister's news. Viola immediately texts the Duke: *'So sorry, my brother rang. He has just come back from a trip to the States. I'm dashing home to see him as it's been so long and he says he has news.'*

The evening sun caresses the surface of the lake as the Duke swims alone. Climbing dripping out of the cool water, he feels in need of company and decides to surprise his young assistant, Seb, and his brother newly returned from the States, and take them on a boys' night out on the town. He recalls his student days and colours his memories with Utopian pleasure. He will take them to his old Oxford haunts and tease out young Seb's inclinations - just for his own amusement, of course. The thought immediately cheers him up.

In the glow of the setting sun and with the sound of cheerful voices and clinking glasses in the background, the producer, Malcolm Vole, dressed as a lady of the night courtesy of a visit to Wardrobe, enters the maze. He looks at his watch. He is a man of precision. It is exactly nine o'clock. But what is this? His eyes are dazzled by a bright light. The floodlights shining on him are so powerful that his eyes begin to water. The sound of hysterical laughter engulfs him and when his vision clears, he sees fingers pointing at him. Wolf whistles echo around the maze.

'Can you believe it? That's Malcolm Voles!'

'And Grayson Perry's on his way - may the best woman win!'

Malcolm usually preens himself with pleasure when in the spotlight but this is utter humiliation. How can it have happened? He looks around. He alone is in fancy dress. He resolves to brazen it out and takes a bow, and then another, and another as he slowly retreats behind a bush. When he turns to run, he collides with a smug Toby Wagstaff. He grabs him by the collar and thrusts him into the hedge.

'Assault and battery? A sacking matter, surely?' says the baritone, grinning in the direction of the wardrobe mistress. Awareness of the checkmate situation spreads across Malcolm's face but he grits his teeth, gives Toby another angry push and makes his way as privately as possible back to his car.

Meanwhile Sir Andrew has followed the unsuspecting Olivia into the maze. He rushes up behind her and puts his hands over her eyes.

'It is I - you know who - the one you have been waiting for.'

Olivia pulls his hands away with a strength that takes him by surprise. She swings around and slaps him across his face.

'Why can't you understand that I just want to be left alone,' she cries. She can't get away quickly enough. All she wants to do is get home...

An hour later as she walks up the steps to the station, Olivia stops suddenly. 'Sebastian, what on earth are you doing here?' she demands.

Sebastian turns and looks at her. 'Sorry, do I know you?' he asks. Then, flushed with embarrassment, he realises he is addressing the angel of the top C, Olivia Jenkinson. He had of course never met her like this, face to face, only admired her from a distance in full costume and stage make up.

'But of course, I do.' He gathers his wits, breaks into his best smile and makes to shake her hand.

'Why are you being so formal? Have you suddenly forgotten all our private conversations?' asks Olivia.

The truth begins to dawn on Sebastian. 'I live near here. Please may I take you home for a drink? There is someone I would very much like you to meet.'

Sitting at the kitchen table in the house on Osney Island with Viola and Sebastian, Olivia tries, in vain, to control her laughter. 'This is no good. I must stop. All this laughter is not good for my voice. You two...' and once more she doubles up as she tries to control herself. At that precise moment there is a knock on the door. Viola goes to answer it.

It is the Duke expecting to sweep two young men off for a night on the tiles. He looks from Viola to Sebastian and back again.

'One face, one voice.' His expression changes from one of incredulity and then to anger as he takes in the situation.

The door opens again and in comes faithful Harry.

'Can anyone join in?' he asks.

Viola bursts into tears. Harry gives her a hug, tenderly wiping her eyes and turns to the Duke.

'Don't be angry with her. She loves her brother and, well, she thinks she loves you too,' he explains.

Viola cries even more then and buries her head in Harry's jumper. He tips her face forward and kisses it with passion.

'And I love her,' he says grinning sheepishly. 'Bit of a mess don't you think!'

The Duke looks at the smiling Olivia and relaxes. Their shared experience of the charming deception draws them into each other's arms. Viola for once is looking deep into Harry's eyes.

Sebastian puts on a CD, not of *Double Jeopardy* by the composer Frederick Glass, but an aria from Mozart's *Cosi fan Tutte:* all forgiveness and reconciliation.

CAT AMONGST THE PIGEONS

MARK DAVIES

What follows is a cat's-eye view of the balloon ascent made by James Sadler and his son, John, on 7 July 1810 as part of Oxford's annual Commemoration Week events.

'Cats can't fly!' If I had a mouse every time I heard that jibe, I'd be a fat cat indeed! 'You're a dimkit!' was the kind of taunt I endured from friends and foes alike. 'You're a furhead! 'You're a kitwit!'

Yet I always knew that I *was* right, that my great-grandfather *had* all those years ago risen into those regions of azure sky and fanciful improbability to fly higher than Oxford's highest tower and beyond her tallest spire. It was not within my power to prove it, though, so I simply had to bear the insults of every blackguard black cat, malevolent moggy, and mouldy mouser with as much dignity as I could muster. Yes, I had to endure the many catcalls - distasteful expression! - and hear myself called cheat, rascal, scoundrel, and even that most catty of all insults: 'Birdbrain!'

But now here I was, alone amidst the boundless fields of ether, as living proof that cats can indeed fly. Mama had told me the story of Great-Grandpa's aerial voyage so often that in truth the prospect I beheld of the unfolded earth below came as little surprise. She had memorised the story told by *her* mother, who had seen the famous ascent from the Physic Garden with her own eyes and heard the account with her own ears. Though much affected while in the upper regions, Great-Grandpa had descended safely to tread the earth again in a nearby meadow, to the great satisfaction of a numerous and respectable company of Oxford's Gentlemen and Ladies, who greatly approved of the enterprise and expressed the highest degree of contentment. Cats *can* fly; they *can*!

I had detected on the previous day that something momentous was afoot. I was not chased away from my favourite adopted household as usual, and the unmistakable air of excitement and nervous anticipation informed me that I was to participate in some great happening, alerted by some seventh sense. (Yes, you, dear reader, may be constrained to five senses, but that which *you* might call 'intuition' is *our* seventh. With our sixth, we cats can sense the ghosts and spectres which flit among you, which steer your destiny, which enter your dreams, and control what you like to call 'luck'.)

Even when it became apparent that the day heralded an emulation of my aeronautical ancestor, I kept the intention most carefully concealed - even from Mama. I feared that otherwise word would spread, and my female acquaintanceship, which is extensive, particularly among the tabbies, would take alarm and be despondent at what they would inevitably perceive as a final farewell, nine lives or not.

It was some time after midday that I allowed myself to be conveyed in my basket through the gathered throngs of the populace. Once inside the car beneath the inflated fabric of the giant globe of the balloon, the noise and fumes, I must confess, caused me some alarm, having never experienced any such thing before in my short life. But I recalled Mama's words, of how Great-Grandpa had also told of his identical terror, three lifetimes earlier, and I distracted myself with a most vigorous licking and preening of my fur.

Soon after, amidst the shouts and huzzas of the numerous spectators, I felt the first signs of elevation. Nothing ventured, I felt disposed not to be an idle observer but to take an active part in the activity in which my companions, the two Mr Sadlers, were engaged. Old Mr Sadler patted me gently upon the head and told me that, as it would be of dangerous consequence to venture out, I should sit still. I am, of course, usually oblivious to the call of authority, except when it suits my purpose, but as the wisdom of his counsel was undeniable, I complied, and began to purr a little tune, to prove both the placidity of my temper and my decreasing fear and apprehension.

We had not travelled far before Mr Sadler produced a bottle of brandy, after which he and his son drank a toast to the University, the City, and Sir Sydney Smith, 'The Conqueror of Bonaparte; the hero of Acre'. The latter gentleman, I came to know, achieved a famous victory, many years before I was born, against the nation which seems as much feared and hated by the English as dogs are by cats. He was, at that very moment, watching us from the ground below.

In the early stages of our journey I distracted myself from the unnerving novelty of my situation by contemplating a means by which to purloin the slices of cold beef which had been stowed on board. These, along with some choice delicacies from the renowned confectionery establishment of Mr Sadler's brother in the High, were placed tantalisingly within my sight, yet just beyond the reach of my outstretched paw. Thus denied, I reverted to preening myself - though, truth be told, not even a tongue's-width of my fur had escaped my earlier attention. Just then, however, Mr Sadler lifted me up to the rim of the car, and I beheld the view.

'Look, Puss,' he said, little knowing that I understood. 'Do you espy those two little specks of villages? Islip and Woodeaton they be called, and the eminence betwixt them is where I first re-trod the welcoming earth, after my very first ascension.'

'There should be a memorial there, father,' said Mr Sadler junior. 'It was such a valiant and intrepid thing that you did. Mr Lunardi has a stone where *he* landed, and that Frenchie Blanchard too, I'm told, over the Channel. 'Tis to the disgrace of the city of your birth, and especially the Gentlemen of the

University, that there is none down there to honour you, the first of our nation ever to fly.'

'Well, perhaps if Puss here lands in the same spot, he'll be better honoured,' was the dry response. 'Is the parachute securely attached?'

Now, this, my friends, was not at all what I had expected, seventh sense or no. When Great-Grandpa had flown, he had remained the whole time inside the sturdy car which hung beneath the balloon. I suddenly perceived that *I* was to be plummeted earthwards with only a frail piece of cloth preventing a plunge into oblivion.

However, I was well aware of Mr Sadler's renown as a skilled fabricator and machinist, as well as an aeronaut. It was he, after all, who had ensured the safe return of Great-Grandpa, 26 years earlier, and it was he that the great newspaper man Mr Jackson had called 'the first to be his own Architect, Engineer, Chemist, and Projector'. And I found the tuneful resonance of Mr Sadler's calm, unhurried voice - quite unlike the clipped accents and loud expostulations to which I was more accustomed among the Oxonian scholars - to be of soothing reassurance.

I was still somewhat alarmed, of course, but I thought of what my tabby admirers might think, should any hint of reluctance somehow find its way to their ears, and I mewed my readiness. Now, I have been used to sudden and discomforting tumbles from the roofs of high buildings and from the elevated boughs of trees, but never before had I experienced so dreadful a shock as the commencement of my fall. Ravaged by wind and cold, I fell with the most alarming velocity, but once the parachute had become fully extended, my downward progress slowed and I was able to enjoy the prospect. It entailed a novel sum of pleasure no words can truly convey - though I shall do my best.

Although the distance cast a certain blurriness over the scene below, yet with my young, sharp eyes I could still discern the meadow from which we had departed, at the back of Merton College. I could see the dark, odorous alleys and passageways of my own familiar haunts; my favourite cooks' shops, where long sojourns were rewarded with the juiciest discarded morsels; and the garbage heaps *par excellence*, where banquets of unwarily bloated mice were almost guaranteed.

I spotted too a gathering of crows on top of Magdalen Tower, and felt myself very superior to be looking down on these competitors for sustenance, to be floating here, an untouchable invader of their own airy domain. Except that, as I suddenly realised, they were not birds at all, but some senior dons and fellows of the college, their black robes fluttering in the wind, and shrunken bird-sized by the deceit of distance.

Likewise the cows in the open fields immediately below me looked no larger than piebald mice - a thought which induced a sudden desire to feast on both milk and rodent. Between the fields a phalanx of people streamed out of the city in pursuit of the Sadlers' balloon. Some walked, some ran, some rode up the London road, trying to gain the most extended possible sighting of the glorious silken sphere, which, I could just detect, was disappearing majestically beyond the eastern horizon.

Once their balloon had vanished from sight, I could see that every eye was turned in my direction. Down and down I went, through a great flock of pigeons which dispersed in all directions at the unexpected incursion by a fearsome and (to all outward appearances) fearless foe. Several ladies swooned, I noted, fearing perhaps that I should descend into the river. To their obvious great joy, however, and my own great relief, my downward journey avoided all such watery dangers and terminated in the sun-dried fields between the villages that I later learned are called Headington and Marston.

Landing was, I confess, an alarming experience: far more

so than any previous experience on that day. I bumped along for some distance, turning head over paws too oft to count, though the bruises received were more to my dignity than to my person. But my ordeal was made more than tolerable by the inexpressible satisfaction of seeing hundreds of birds thrown into twittering, squawking confusion as I careered through their many unsuspecting flocks, like some angelic visitation on their final day of judgement, scattering them in terror unutterable.

My wind-blown progress terminated in a hawthorn hedge. There I waited, confident that with so very many anxious observers I should not have to remain entrapped for long. I was indeed correct: it was but a matter of moments before a countryman arrived to assess my wellbeing. From there he swiftly conveyed me to the nearest road. There he paused, seeming uncertain what to do next, and a large crowd quickly gathered.

'What's writ on the label on his collar?' I heard a man ask, but when he poked his fingers towards me, I rewarded him, I regret to say, with a hiss and a bite and a scratch. My nerves were, you understand, most decidedly and understandably jangled. His nonetheless coaxing words persuaded me of his good intentions, so I quietened myself and heard him announce: 'For delivery to Miss Bobart, High-street, Oxford'.

My destination decided, I enjoyed a hero's journey back into Oxford - and justly so, if I may make so bold! I was cooed and clucked at by everyone we passed, the road being crammed with every species of conveyance, from the titled equipage to the humble handcart, and every form of humanity, from the grandest nobleman to the lowliest vagabond. On our way it took but little persuasion for my courier - I never learned his name, but let us call him Porter - to stop and exhibit me to the concerned and the curious. Again and again he stopped to pull back the curtain of the parachute, for anyone willing to part with a penny. I consoled myself at this affront to my sensibilities with the hope - unfulfilled, I fear - that some of these coppers might find their way to old Mr Sadler, that most ingenious but unfortunate man, for whose benefit a subscription had been opened at Seale's and Dickeson's coffee houses to defray the costs of his great aerial undertaking.

I remember only one of the hundreds of faces which gawped at me during our progress. It belonged to a youth who came up to us in a great agitation, claiming to be another of Mr Sadler's sons. He had walked all the way from London to witness his father's great moment, he said, with but a few pence in his pocket, but, arriving too late, would now perforce be obliged to walk straight back again. At least seeing the cat was a small compensation, he added, miserably but stoically. He told the truth, my senses told me, and I was pleased to note that Porter thought so too, and that he pressed one of his many newly acquired pennies into the boy's hand, to help him on his way.

By the time we reached the High, the coins in Porter's pocket chinked ever more heavily, and our pace became ever slower. At every coach office there was uproar, with people fighting one another for a place, now that the week's entertainment had concluded. Many windows were broken, and many bones too, I wouldn't wonder, but eventually we stopped outside a station opposite Queen's College, where Porter fought his way forward, and we recommended ourselves to the attention of the coachmaster, for clearly it was he, Mr Bobart himself, standing authoritatively by a packed coach next to a sign which proclaimed:

> If an excursion by coach you desire,
> To Bobart apply, at his office well known,
> Day and night there are many drive coaches for hire,
> But he has the pleasure of driving his own!

On reading the label which was still on my lovely red collar, Mr Bobart ushered us the few feet to the entrance of his dwelling house next to the Alfred Head Inn. Once there he bellowed, 'Anna? Charlotte? Are you there? Come, daughters, and see what has fallen from the sky and into your laps.' Two young girls came rushing to the porch and stared at me with undisguised joy.

'You remember that strange old gentlemen you met yesterday? The one whom you doubted when his son said they were set to walk the air and sweep the cobwebs from the sky? Well, see, he has sent you a little furry angel from the heavens. Now, show this fellow inside, daughters, and hasten to tell your mother.' So saying, he felt in his pocket for a coin to reward my already much-rewarded Porter. '*Felix fugit et tempus fugit!*' he added, chuckling, and stooped to kiss both his daughters. 'I must away - away from the pandemonium which assails us. Tune up your tin, Bill,' I heard him proclaim over the hubbub. Moments later a shrill bugle sounded, there was the crack of a whip, a whinny of horses, a theatrical expostulation by Mr Bobart in which I could only discern the repeated word '*Londinium*', and they were off. And so was I, off to a new life, so different from my old, as the adored and pampered companion of the Misses Bobart.

After the stress of the ordeal and of my hero's welcome, I had thought that I might be left in peace the next day, but not a bit of it. I did find time to scratch these words, while the details were fresh in my mind, but back in my basket, I found myself placed in full view at a banquet in honour of the two Mr Sadlers, who had returned that afternoon from St Gertrude knows where. The envious and disconcerted looks of my disbelieving friends were some compensation for this indignity, and I soon warmed to the attention, especially when I heard myself immortalised in song by Mr Pinkney. Here, let me purr the relevant verse to you:

> Now they soar aloft, all the Ladies smitten,
> Down comes the parachute and Miss Bobart's Kitten.
> Genius ne'er can want Englishmen's best Boons, Sirs,
> Here's the English Aëronaut, King of all Balloons, Sirs.

Mama tells me that when I heard this, my satisfied grin would have done credit to our Cheshire brethren, and that I resembled the renowned cat burglar whose appropriation of all of the cream from every college buttery within spitting distance of Catte Street one gloriously glutinous night, is a thing of legend, celebrated throughout all catdom.

So now my days are spent basking in the fame of being both the valiant companion of the 'King of all Balloons' and the handsome ward of the daughters of Oxford's 'Classical Coachman'. With no need to fend for myself on the streets, or to demean myself by foraging for food, I spend much of my new leisure time musing on the use to which balloons and parachutes might be applied in pursuit of the feathered race. One day I hope to explain my theories to Mr Sadler, that most skilled but oppressed of mechanics. He, though, seems disinclined to return to the city of his birth, perhaps because he has been so harshly used, out of pique and jealousy of his superior science. One thing is sure, though: popular opinion varies as with the wind, and never again would any doubting Tom dare to say to me: 'Cats can't fly!'

FLYING WITH THE ANGELS

JANE GORDON-CUMMING

Christmas Eve! Mary Aldridge's heart raced with excitement as the train puffed northwards. Soon she would be seeing her mother and little sisters again. She clutched the small parcels she had for them - not that she could afford much on a servant girl's wages, but she knew the girls would love the rag dolls from Oxford market, and her mother would treasure the needle-case she had spent the evenings embroidering, up in her attic room.

The carriage was crowded, full of chattering passengers, everyone, like her, excited at the thought of seeing loved ones for Christmas. Mary had managed to get a seat by the window, and she pressed her nose against the glass, glad to be in this safe, warm world on such a cold day. There was the canal she sometimes walked beside on her afternoon off. Smoke rose from the chimney of the cottage beside Duke's Cut, but the lock, which should have been lively with people and horses, was eerily still today, the barges lying motionless, imprisoned in their moorings by the thick ice. This wouldn't be a good Christmas for boatmen's families. How lucky she was to have steady work in the large Banbury Road house, and employers who were kind enough to spare her for the holiday.

Lesley Davenant checked her list again - at least the second time since the train had left Banbury. Had she forgotten anyone? Too late now. Oh dear, she did hope that computer game was the one Gary had meant. The shop in Castle Quay had said she could change it after Christmas, but it was a long way to come back from Oxford if it turned out she'd bought the wrong thing. Maybe this last minute shopping trip hadn't been a good idea, with such a lot to do for tomorrow. Must remember to get the turkey in from the garden shed, and defrost the cream cheese for the starter. Would everyone be happy with salmon mousse? She had a feeling Alan's sister wasn't very keen on fish, come to think of it. Better make her something else. Christmas was such a stressful time, getting everything right for everybody.

She gazed out at the frozen landscape, trying to dismiss a pervading feeling of unease. It was beautiful, this part of the Cherwell valley, the canal and the river weaving sometimes apart, sometimes together. The scene ahead might have come straight from a Christmas card: Shipton, with its pretty church by the bridge, Hampton Gay church opposite, alone in its deserted fields, and the picturesque ruins of the manor, gaunt among the trees. Why couldn't she just relax and enjoy this lovely view? Anyone else would be looking forward to Christmas Day. There was nothing more she could do, sitting here on a train, and anyway, tomorrow would probably go swimmingly. …Yet still Lesley couldn't rid herself of the conviction that something terrible was about to happen.

Mary loved being in the train, flying along behind the engine wrapped in a cloud of steam. This must be how the angels felt as they flew across the sky, looking down on all the people below. The train whistled a warning and they rattled over a level crossing. She caught a glimpse of a little hump-backed bridge with a lock beyond, frozen and deserted. A man in a farm cart was waiting for them to go by, on his way to take extra food to those sheep in the fields on the other side of the line. She felt sorry for him, out there in the cold instead of in the nice warm train. Farmers had to tend their stock whatever the weather, poor things.

Damn, what was the hold up? With a slow squeal of brakes, the train had made one of those mysterious stops in the middle of nowhere that trains are prone to. They had ground to a halt in some wretched industrial estate in Kidlington. In growing frustration, Lesley watched the cars shooting past on the main road, and fantasised about leaping out and catching a bus. It could only be about ten minutes to Oxford.

Ah, this must be what they were waiting for. A steam train was approaching on the other line - a Christmas excursion for railway buffs from Didcot, no doubt. Lesley turned to watch it go past, fascinated in spite of herself, a little surprised that no one else in the carriage seemed interested. What a strange collection of stock they'd put together - two steam engines, with a funny little old carriage in between, and then a guard's van before the rest of the carriages. It was as if they'd taken up a challenge to use every exhibit in the Railway Museum. This train was stopping too. It drew up beside her, enveloping everything in a great cloud of steam.

Good heavens, they had gone to town! The train itself might look a bit odd, but the carriages were full to bursting, and every passenger was dressed in authentic looking Victorian costume, without a single trendy hair-cut or pair of modern glasses to spoil the illusion. These steam buffs really did like to do things properly. A girl of about fourteen was sitting in the carriage opposite, her cheeks rosy under a wide-brimmed hat, her eyes bright with excitement. Lesley felt a sudden pang of envy for the girl's ability to give herself up to such frank, unadulterated pleasure. This child wasn't weighed down with responsibilities at Christmas. Nothing to do but enjoy her trip on a steam train, and look forward to further delights tomorrow.

Across the crowded carriage Mary could just read the name above the platform: 'Woodstock Road'. That was the station for Kidlington, wasn't it? She didn't know why the express had paused here. The passengers glanced at each other, but no one alighted, and there was certainly no room for anyone else to squeeze in.

Mary turned back to her own window, and saw that another train had drawn up next to theirs. How pretty! Instead of the familiar cream and brown, it was a gay red and silver. They must have done it like that specially for Christmas. The lady in the carriage opposite her seemed very thinly dressed for this cold day. She wore no hat over her dark hair, and her scarf was little more than a flimsy handkerchief knotted round her neck. Yet she didn't look poor. Her face was smooth, more like a lady's than someone who worked for a living, and her lips were coloured an unreal cherry red. Mary pursed her own unadorned lips. She knew what kind of women painted their faces. Nevertheless, there was something about this stranger which claimed her attention. In contrast to the gaily decorated carriage she rode in, the woman wore an anxious frown, as if all the cares of the world were on her shoulders. Why did she look so unhappy on Christmas Eve? As her train began to move away from theirs, Mary gave the sad lady a friendly smile, trying to encourage her to forget her troubles, if only for a day.

Hm, cheeky madam! - Grinning at her in that 'cheer up, it may never happen' way. Christmas *was* going to happen, whether Lesley was ready or not. It wasn't something one could postpone till one was more in the mood. And there was no denying, she couldn't have been less in the mood.

She tried to talk sense into herself, as the train gathered speed. Even if the meal wasn't perfect, and the presents not precisely what everybody wanted, they would probably still have a very nice time. No one else around seemed to have this gloomy attitude to Christmas. Every window in that housing-estate showed cheerful coloured lights and glittering trees. Even that guy trundling over the hump-backed bridge in a tractor had tied a sprig of holly to his cab, poor sod. At least she didn't have a job which involved being outside in the cold every day.

But counting her blessings didn't seem to be doing Lesley any good. As they rumbled over the crossing with the road from the Garden Centre, the feeling of dread became almost overwhelming.

Off again across the fields! It was like a ride at St. Giles's Fair, Mary thought, but one that went on and on. The boatmens' village of Thrupp was eerily quiet, its line of barges waiting for the thaw, its wharf still and silent. There was the little church beside the railway line and the old manor house in the trees beyond, all that was left of the village of Hampton Gay. What kind of Christmas party would they be having in the manor, the lords and ladies? But Mary didn't envy them. She was superior to the whole of mankind, flying past in her train. Almost she felt they were about to take off into the sky. How wonderful that would be! Soaring up to heaven to go and meet the angels.

...What was happening? For one glorious moment it seemed that her dream had come true. Mary found herself flying through the air, free of the train and the rest of the world. She didn't feel the bang, or the icy water. By the time her carriage sank into the freezing canal, her soul was already with the angels.

Lesley wasn't sure when the oppression began to lift, all she knew was that she suddenly felt a lot better. Perhaps it was the sight of the Oxford ring road ahead, the psychological boundary of home. Didn't the canal down there at Duke's Cut make a lovely winter's scene? - the lock, and its white cottage and the arching brick bridge. They should come up here for their Christmas walk tomorrow. ...Oh come on, it was all going to be fine. Why not relax and look forward to the day, instead of worrying about things that might never happen? That young girl in the other train had the right attitude. Make the most of the moment, and enjoy life while you had the chance.

Historical Notes

On 24th December 1874 a train came off the rails at Shipton-on-Cherwell and 34 people lost their lives.

WELCOME TO NORTH OXFORD

ALISON HONEY

Martin had made it - made his money on the trading floor, said goodbye to the City and was looking forward to very early retirement in a large semi-detached Victorian house on - as the smug estate agent had described it - 'one of the most sought-after roads in North Oxford'. Plenty of room for his plasma TV over the period fireplace. All that was missing was a place to park his black Maserati, but he would soon sort that. There was a good-sized front garden. Just a bit of planning procedure to get through, then tick, done.

Two weeks had gone by and no one had asked him in for a drink or knocked on the door to welcome him. He had run into a few of the residents on the street on his way out to walk his dog but once they'd clocked his Essex accent they cooled off. When he mentioned that he was putting in an application for off-street parking their reaction was positively glacial. He had made a mental note that Julia Penrose from number 11 with her cold grey eyes and firm opinions was a particular piece of work.

People didn't seem to say hello here. They didn't meet his eye unless they wanted to tell him he was doing something wrong like using a co-op plastic bag instead of one of those weird feeling biodegradable ones to pick up the dog mess. Last week he'd been taken aback as an old tramp with wild snowy hair had actually stopped him on his walk along the canal to start a conversation, admired his dog and asked him his pet's name. It was the first remotely friendly encounter he'd experienced since moving in and Martin had felt a warm feeling towards the old bloke. On replying 'Dexter' the tramp raised one of his overgrown eyebrows quizzically in response. It was then Martin realised he was probably not a tramp at all but a professor...

'Oh, looking for his companion, Sinister?'

What did that mean? Must be some sort of upmarket BBC drama, Dexter and Sinister, like Morse and Lewis, He'd heard of them. But his instinct told him it was a test - a way of pigeon-holing him - and to find out if he 'belonged'. He could tell by the way the old man peered over his glasses, those cunning steely eyes waiting for a reaction, like a terrier about to jump a rabbit.

He began to wish he'd moved to Headington. There was a shark in someone's roof there.

'What do they mean "oasis"? It's a weed-filled grubby patch where all the neighbourhood cats and foxes hang out and do their business. And it's only an "oasis" because the rest of the street have paved over their front gardens already. They're making out like I'm destroying half the bloody Amazonian rainforest!' Martin slammed down the phone on his architect.

Having logged on to the Oxford City Council planning page to see how the application to convert his front garden to off-street parking was progressing Martin was dumbfounded to see that not only had every household in the street written a letter of objection but, as if that wasn't enough, they'd then all got together and signed a joint letter too. It was like a military pincer movement and he knew full well who was behind it.

Sure enough four weeks later Martin got the news that the planning application had been rejected. His architect hinted that someone on the committee may have been lent on - or had 'a special relationship' with one of the members. It seemed as if the Mafia was lurking behind the leafy plane trees of North Oxford. Next thing he'd be waking up to a horse's head on his pillow.

Julia, aged forty-eight, inhabitant of the City of Oxford (North) for the past ten years, had climbed the greasy pole of the local property market and had now reached the top (excluding any house north of the Banbury Road within spitting distance of the Dragon School which was beyond even her wildest dreams). She was now the proud owner (no need to mention the mortgage) of an HW Moore house nestled between Woodstock Road and Jericho. She had arrived.

However, the arrival of Martin was a fly in the ointment. Ever since the Saville's sold sign had gone up and the removal van had trundled off taking the detritus of thirty years of the retiring Professor and his wife to a home in the Cotswolds, Julia had been waiting on tenterhooks to discover the identity and more importantly the background of the new owner of number 15. She had been hoping for at least some BBC presenter (ITV at a stretch) or perhaps a successful author or an actor but a financial 'trader' had been well down Julia's list. Not for the first time she felt a tinge of regret that she (well, her husband) had not been able to stretch to a house on the crescent in Park Town. That would have been a different ball game altogether.

However, the tipping point was the planning application. Martin needed to be taught a lesson on how things were done in North Oxford. Rules were to be observed. That is how she found herself striding purposefully up the four steps to Martin's front door. She recoiled at the smell of gloss paint and even more at the sight of the freshly painted orange door. She made a mental note to inform the Victorian Society of a possible colour infringement. She pressed the buzzer (ditto infringement) and shuddered as she heard the polyphonic ring tone of 'London Bridge is Falling Down' chiming inside.

Martin paused the TV, shuffled to the door, peered

through the peep hole and reeled back seeing Julia's distorted image - even scarier through the fish-eye lens. He took a deep breath and unlatched the door.

'Hi Julia, what can I do for you?'

'Martin I was just wondering if you'd had any news of your planning application?'

Julia tossed her head, smiled an unnerving wolf-like grin and fixed her steely grey eyes on Martin's face.

'Yep all went through without a hitch. Starting work next week.'

Julia's affected smile crumpled. Martin enjoyed the moment.

'Only joking. It was turned down.'

Julia's face relaxed as much as it could. She looked Martin in the eye and spoke with exaggerated sympathy, 'Oh I'm SO sorry.'

Lying hypocrite, Martin thought.

She carried on regardless. 'They're so strict aren't they? But there are rules to be observed and after all we should know that, as the privileged owners of properties in the North Oxford Victorian Suburb Conservation Area.' She delivered the last six words in hushed reverential tones. 'We have a responsibility to protect the integrity of the area.'

Martin responded, tongue firmly in cheek, 'Oh well, let's look on the bright side. I just love that tingle of excitement not knowing where I'm going to park every time I come home, and walking from those far-flung Walton Manor parking permit spaces has to be good for my waistline, Do you know, I've lost half a stone since moving here?'

It was water off a duck's back.

'And you'll still have your *lonicera*,' Julia volunteered.

What the hell is that? thought Martin. Sounds like a nasty foot infection.

Julia pounced on his horticultural ignorance.

'Honeysuckle. Now Martin, I know you may be feeling

a little disappointed but this could be the start of something wonderful. I have a friend, Persephone Hawkins, who's VERY highly thought of in the garden design world, and she could make your front garden look much more attractive. More in keeping with the period and the neighbourhood?'

She was a serial interferer. Not content with sabotaging his planning application she was standing on HIS doorstep and telling HIM shamefacedly what to do with HIS property.

'Thanks Julia, but I've got the garden design taken care of. It was one of the first things I did once I heard the decision.'

Julia smiled patronisingly. 'So you won't be needing Persephone's number then?'

He shook his head. No he bloody well wouldn't.

Thursday morning two weeks later Julia sat at her kitchen table with the latest edition of the Oxford Times. It was her weekly ritual and while sipping her coffee she scanned the pages listing the new planning applications to see if any needed her 'attention'. Opening the paper to the relevant section her eyes were immediately drawn to an address. Her address. An application for a three-storey glass rear extension and a basement to house a home cinema and gym. An Iceberg.

Horrified, she clasped her hand to her mouth. Grabbing the phone she punched the keys to ring the planning department (a number she knew off by heart); she would make someone pay for this appalling mistake.

'What do you mean? That's ridiculous!' Julia slammed down the phone in disgust.

Grabbing the paper, she flew up the basement stairs, flung open her front door, slammed it shut and strode furiously down the street to Martin's house. She jammed her finger on the buzzer.

Hearing the bell chime Martin smiled to himself and made his way to the door. He opened it gently to see an incandescent Julia shaking on his doorstep.

'Oh hello Julia, everything OK? What can I do for you?'

'Well, you can explain this for a start,' she barked, waving an increasingly crumpled copy of the Oxford Times in his face. 'Do you realise what you've done to my reputation? I could be expelled from the Victorian Society!'

Martin had rehearsed his response.

'Well, Julia, as you seem to be so familiar with the planning process you should know that you don't have to own a property to put in a planning application. You just have to pay for it and as you know I've got no problem with money. Just a bit of fun...'

He closed the door on a speechless Julia and went back to his TV with a satisfied smile on his face.

The following day Julia was woken by the repeated beeping of a reversing lorry. She peered at her bedside alarm clock and was disappointed to see that it was within the designated starting time for construction work so there would be no chance of submitting a complaint. However, curiosity got the better of her and she climbed out of bed and peered through a chink in her Osborne & Little curtains. A truck towing a flat-bed trailer was tentatively manoeuvring its way between the parked cars lining the road. Julia squinted - its cargo appeared to be a life-size model of a dromedary painted in day-glo pink.

She watched bewildered as the truck ground to a halt outside number 15. The driver lumbered out of the cab and wrapped a canvas sling around the camel's midriff. He pulled it tight and once satisfied he clambered back in to the lorry. The cargo gradually rose from the trailer bed until it dangled hesitantly over the round-topped Victorian wall. The driver directed the load until it was gently lowered on to Martin's front garden, coming to a rest amidst the tangle of overgrown honeysuckle.

Something was written on the camel's side in bright green. Julia staggered back to her bedside table and fumbled to grab her glasses. She returned to the window and her eyes gradually focused on the lettering.

'Martins Oasis'

She gasped in horror. There was NO apostrophe.

About the Authors

Angela Cecil Reid is currently working on a biography of the Tyssen-Amherst and Mitford families. Her short story *Arthur's Boy* was commended in the Sid Chaplin Short Story Competition, and the opening chapters of her novel for Young Adults, *Nile Cat* reached the regional short list for Waterstone's Wow Factor Competition. She was previously a teacher, working with dyslexic children, and now divides her time between writing and shepherding her rare breed Cotswold sheep on her farm outside Oxford.
www.angelacecilreid.com
www.amherstsofdidlington.com

Gina Claye has recently published a children's poetry book, *English Spelling is Bonkers - Fun Poems to help you Spell*. Other poems have been published in anthologies by Oxford University Press and Scholastic. Her book, *Don't Let Them Tell You How to Grieve*, is used by Cruse Bereavement Care to help those who are grieving. Both *English Spelling is Bonkers* and *Don't Let Them Tell You How to Grieve* are available on Amazon. She is editor of *Compassion*, the journal of The Compassionate Friends (an organisation of bereaved parents, siblings and grandparents supporting those similarly bereaved). She gives talks on parental bereavement to the Hospice movement and Cruse and other similar organisations, and can be contacted at:
gina.claye@icloud.com
www.ginaclaye.co.uk

Mark Davies is an Oxford local historian, guide, and public speaker whose biography of James Sadler and his sons, *'King of all Balloons': The Adventurous Life of James Sadler, The First*

English Aeronaut was published in 2015. It marks a change of element from his main interest in the social and cultural importance of Oxford's waterways, on which subject he has published a number of local interest titles. See:
www.oxfordwaterwalks.co.uk

Jane Gordon-Cumming has published numerous short stories, including three in previous OxPens anthologies and a collection of ghost stories set on the Oxford Canal. Her romantic comedy, *A Proper Family Christmas*, is currently out with Accent Press, and *A Real Family Holiday* is in the pipeline. She is also writing the history of her grandparents: Sir William Gordon Cumming of the Baccarat Scandal and the American heiress Florence Garner, her proposal for which won the Biographers' Club's Tony Lothian Prize. After many years in Oxfordshire, she and her husband have recently moved to Minchinhampton.
janegordoncumming.wordpress.com

Liz Harris is the author of the historical novels *The Road Back* (US Coffee Time & Romance Book of the Year 2012), *A Bargain Struck* (shortlisted for the RoNA Historical 2013), and the novella, *A Western Heart*. In addition, she has written two contemporary novels, *Evie Undercover* and *The Art of Deception*. Her latest historical novel, *The Lost Girl*, is set in SW Wyoming in the 1870s and 1880s. Liz has also had several short stories published in anthologies. In addition to being an active member of the Historical Novel Society and the Romantic Novelists' Association, Liz's interests are theatre, travelling, reading, and cryptic crosswords. You can visit her website at
www.lizharrisauthor.com

Alison Honey worked in the Publications Department of the National Trust in various editorial and writing roles involving the Handbook, Magazine and Children's publications. She also wrote eight titles for the National Trust's *Investigating* series of non-fiction history books for children. She was commissioned by the Ashmolean to write two guides to coincide with the opening of the new building. *My Ashmolean Discovery Book* (2010) won the Association of Cultural Enterprise's award for best children's publication and *Floor by Floor, a general guide to the galleries*, was published the following year. Alison divides her time between living in Oxford and Singapore. '*Welcome to North Oxford*' is Alison's first published work of fiction.

John Kitchen's first book, *Nicola's Ghost* (New Generation Press) won the New Generation Publishing Prize 2011 and The Writer's Digest Best Self-published Young Adult Novel in the same year. His second book *A Spectre in the Stones* was published by Thames River Press in June 2013 and a third Young Adult novel *Jax' House* was published by Union Bridge Books in May 2016. He also published a Picture Book for younger Children, *Kamazu's Big Swing Band* (New Generation Press) in 2014. Born in Cornwall John graduated from London University and taught in Cornwall, Worcestershire and Oxfordshire until he left teaching to concentrate on writing in 2002.

www.johnkitchenauthor.com

Linora Lawrence has written for The Lady, The Oxford Times and for over twenty years has written features for its monthly magazine, Oxfordshire Limited Edition. Most notably a bi-monthly series of articles entitled *An A – Z of the Bodleian Library* which ran for a year between March 2014 and 2015. She has lived in Oxford for over thirty years during which time she has worked at St Hilda's and Trinity colleges, the Bodleian Library and Oxford University Press. She also worked for Williams Formula 1 where she experienced

a totally different, but fascinating, other world. She now realises that many of the people she has met in Oxford over the past years have unknowingly contributed to the tales she tells, for which she thanks them wholeheartedly.
www.linoralawrence.com

Radmila May was an undergraduate at St Hugh's College where she read Law. She lived in Oxford from 1987 to 2010 except for a seven-year break when she lived in Holland. She now lives in Chiswick but comes back to Oxford to the Writers' Group. She has written articles for the political and literary journal *Contemporary Review* on such subjects as Barbara Pym, the Yugoslav War Crimes Tribunal and a survey of Oxford-set crime fiction (Murder Most Oxford). She has recently co-edited the sixth edition of her late husband's text book, *Criminal Evidence*. She has contributed numerous reviews and articles to the crime fiction e-zine *Mystery People*. This is her third story for the Oxpens short story anthologies.

Ben McSeoin (Mc-Shown) has been writing - in one way or another - for as long as he can remember. In 2011 he gained a Diploma in Literature and Creative Writing with The Open University. *The Day the Snow Fell* is his second short story, his first being *The Beast of Summertown* - found in OxPens' preceding anthology *The Midnight Press and Other Oxford Stories*. His interests include travelling, music, languages and foreign and art-house cinema.

Paul W. Nash is a librarian, bibliographer and book-designer who worked at the Bodleian and at various college libraries in Oxford, and at the British Architectural Library in London. He co-edited *The Private Library* between 1993 and 2008, is currently editor of the Journal of the *Printing Historical Society*, and has written on private presses, the Folio Society, and other aspects of printing and publishing history. He taught printing history, theory and practice at the Bodleian between 2005 and 2015, and is an amateur composer and author of fiction and humorous verse.

Rosie Orr lives in Oxford. Since winning the South Bank Show poetry competition she has had work published in several magazines and anthologies, including *The Virago Book of Love Poetry*, a *PEN Anthology* and *WOW! 366!* She has a short story in each of OWG's four earlier anthologies, and has written and directed a short film, *Let Nothing You Dismay*, which was screened at London's Portobello Film Festival. Her novel *Something Blue* (Contemporary Women's Fiction) was published recently by Accent Press.

Margaret Pelling has lived in Oxford since she was a physics student in the nineteen sixties. Her two published contemporary novels are *A Diamond in the Sky* (Honno) and *Work for Four Hands* (Starborn Books). She is looking for a publisher for another contemporary novel, *The Man Who Walks by the Sea*, and is now writing a historical novel set during the aftermath of the battle of Trafalgar, entitled *Trafalgar's Other Admiral*. This follows the defeated French admiral through his experiences as a prisoner of war in Britain. Maritime history has always been a passion, and her story in this volume reflects that interest. Another Napoleonic prisoner of war is a main character, this time a much younger junior officer of a swashbuckling disposition. Fiction is Margaret Pelling's third 'career'. First came research astrophysics and then the Civil Service, but she's finally found what she wants to do.
www.margaretpelling.co.uk

Andrew Puckett grew up on his parents' farm in Wiltshire. Since then, he has worked in hospital laboratories in

Taunton and London, and was for 15 years Microbiologist in Oxford Blood Transfusion Centre. It was here that he started writing, using these experiences in his first Medical Thriller *Bloodstains*. Ten further novels followed, published mostly by Collins and Constable. He now lives in Taunton with his wife and daughters. Most of his books, backlist and new, have now been published in e-form by Endeavour Press; the last one, *Bed of Nails* being set in Oxford. More are to follow, both in e and print. His books are available on Amazon.

Heather Rosser has always been interested in history and social justice. Her First World War novel, *In the Line of Duty,* is based on her grandfather's experiences as a seaplane pilot and was shortlisted for the RNA Joan Hessayon debut novel award. Her time-slip story in this anthology uses fiction to show a disturbing time in Oxford's recent history. She worked as a teacher in West Africa and was a journalist in Botswana as well as writing articles on childcare for British magazines. Since moving to Oxford, she has written text books for schools in Africa and the Caribbean and is currently working on a memoir of her time in Nigeria.
www.heatherrosser.com

Jane Stemp's degree from Somerville College focused on English language and literature from Beowulf to Chaucer, and was followed by the College of Librarianship Wales postgraduate Diploma in Librarianship. Jane worked for twelve years in an assortment of Oxford University libraries, during which time her novel *Secret Songs* (1997) was shortlisted by the Guardian Children's Book Prize. She is now Historic Collections Librarian for the Institute of Naval Medicine in Gosport, but remains in touch with Oxford Writers Group, and has contributed to all of the Oxford Stories volumes. Jane has also written medical history articles for scientific journals and online sites, and makes occasional media and conference appearances.

Sylvia Vetta is best known for her journalism, public speaking and for her 6 non-fiction books. The last in her castaway series *Oxford Castaways 3* was published in 2017 by Oxfordfolio on behalf of Sobell House. Her first novel, *Brushstrokes in Time*, was published by Claret Press in 2016. For the first time in fiction it shows the courageous birth of the Stars Art Movement in Beijing in 1979. A fictitious artist, Little Winter's haunting story connects us to this time of hope for freedom of expression in China and to the man she loves who is frustrated by being kept 'in small shoes'. It has been turned into an audiobook by Essential Audiobooks (New York) & will be translated into German by Drachenhaus Verlag. Contact Sylvia:
sylviavetta@gmail.com,
https://www.sylviavetta.co.uk or
https://www.facebook.com/SylviaVettaWriter/

Lightning Source UK Ltd.
Milton Keynes UK
UKOW04f1004070817
306828UK00001B/3/P